THE DIARY OF
SARAH
FORBES
BONETTA

A Novel

THE DIARY OF
SARAH
FORBES
BONETTA
A Novel

VICTORIA PRINCEWILL

SCHOLASTIC

A note to readers:
The language used in this book, while accurate to the time, does not include the most offensive terms – or 'n-words' – that would have been used regularly at the time. Although those words are not repeated in this book, it is important to acknowledge that Sarah, and so many others, would have been subjected to such hate speech throughout their lives, and that many people are still.

Published in the UK by Scholastic, 2023
1 London Bridge, London, SE1 9BG
Scholastic Ireland, 89E Lagan Road, Dublin Industrial Estate, Glasnevin, Dublin, D11 HP5F

Text © Victoria Princewill, 2023
Cover illustration © Jael Umerah-Makelemi

The right of Victoria Princewill and Jael Umerah-Makelemi to be identified as the author and illustrator of this work has been asserted by them under the Copyright, Designs and Patents Act 1988.

ISBN 978 07023 1148 2

A CIP catalogue record for this book is available from the British Library.

Printed and bound by CPI Group (UK) Ltd, Croydon, CR0 4YY
Paper made from wood grown in sustainable forests and other controlled sources.

1 3 5 7 9 10 8 6 4 2

www.scholastic.co.uk

"For the ones who are told to speak only when spoken to and then are never spoken to."

- Anis Mojgani

17 August 1860
The Rectory, Palm Cottage
Gillingham, England

I do not like surprises.

There is not a lot that is known about me. When I was born. Who was there. How many siblings I may or may not have had.

Learning about myself is a constant surprise.

Often there is nothing new to learn. No insight to be found. A few days ago, it was my birthday. Or rather, it was the day my first caretaker, Mrs Phipps, a member of the Queen's household, had chosen to celebrate annually as my birthday. How was it chosen? Well, in England, we do as the Englishman would. Where there is no truth, we invent a story!

And four days on from my invented birthday, I am here, curled in my bed at close to midnight, scribbling in this little diary all that happened that day. How shall I address those moments I cannot remember? As the Englishman would?

Let us begin with what I know about myself. The question of invention need not arise just yet.

My name is Forbes.

Sarah Forbes Bonetta. I was born in West Africa and later kid-napped by King Ghezo of Dahomey, who murdered the rest of my family and kept me alive to be a human sacrifice. I was rescued by the Royal Navy captain Frederick Forbes, who persuaded the king to present me as a gift to the Queen of the British Empire. Forbes is the one who named me. 'Sarah Forbes Bonetta' is entirely his creation. He gave me his surname and then the surname of his ship ... he had me baptized as Sarah when we arrived in England. As to what alchemy led him to name me thus, the mystery died with the man. I was Etta to the girls in Sierra Leone, Sally to the Queen, Sarah Bonetta to the reverend and his family, and – whether it was four days ago, or in fact today, or some day in the future or the distant past – I will at some point be or have turned seventeen. And today is the day I have chosen to write about it, as the day comes to an end.

I have been told many times that I am a girl with too many opin-ions. But I am not interested in limiting my own voice. Today is the day I decided that I shall be the one to write the story of my life, so I can recall who I am, who I have been, and how I have grown, simply by returning to my very own words. And they will not be frivolous. I shall write who I am, how I lived, what took place. This will be a sphere of history as much as memory – a gift to myself, to honour that which I lost and cannot replace.

On the subject of that which I have lost, I should tell how I came to be *here*, living with Reverend Schoen and his wife, Elizabeth, in Kent, following the captain's death. It was the captain's wife, dear Mary Forbes, who informed the Queen of my cough. At the time, the Queen became convinced this rather awful weather was the cause. While other Africans have apparently moved to England and thrived, I had this persistent cough that all the fires in Windsor Castle could not abate. Poor Mary was opposed to my leaving and, alas, I have not seen her since I returned. Still, her concerns about my health were acted upon. And like a parcel being returned, back to Africa I was shipped.

I was sent to the Female Institution, a school for African girls in Freetown, Sierra Leone, run by missionaries in the region. I boarded the ship some months after Captain Forbes' passing. It was summer in England, which does not mean all that much, but it was a beautiful June day that I stepped onto the HMS *Bathurst*. I did not wish to go to Africa and did not enjoy myself much there, but this is by the by. I was favoured by the missionaries and teachers, and I did well, because work is a useful distraction from grief. I learned that the previous year, as I settled in the Forbeses' home. Although, with the captain's family, *play* proved as glorious a distraction from grief or pain as work itself. I was in Sierra Leone for four years. In 1855, I was returned here, to England. I do not know what the reasoning was for my being placed with the Schoens, as opposed to the Forbes family once more, but I suspect that the Queen wanted me to stay in

England, and Mrs Forbes had retired to Scotland. The Schoens live in Gillingham, Kent, and have seven children. The Forbeses' home was grand and with the children there was always merriment to be had. The Schoens' home is comparatively modest, unfit for a family of nine. My presence makes ten, and I have not counted the cook or the nursemaid.

I am not unhappy here. The Reverend James Schoen is studious; he speaks many African languages and likes to read. He talks to me at length about any new scholarly book he purchases and I do not resent these conversations, nor that he expects me to have a certain level of aptitude. I seem to not only match his requirement but surpass it too. His eldest children Frederick and Annie have different, if amusing, relationships with me. Frederick, when younger, would follow me around incessantly. It was tiresome from the beginning; I suspect he was my first admirer! Annie was quite the opposite. Her manner to me is cool. I am not concerned, as Mrs Schoen's manner is so emotive and engaged that, after a single conversation, I find myself yearning for Annie's cool indifference, just as I might seek some extended time alone. One might assume that such a maternal woman would have taken great pains to craft the optimal birthday but, alas, it was not to be. Each year I have found it disappointing, but this year, with promises mounted high and seventeen being such a profound age, so close to responsibility and adulthood, I was excited for it.

I was a fool, of course.

But what better way to mark turning seventeen than to bury your childhood self?

Let me tell you what I was expecting: I would rise early and feel the warm sunlight on my face. I would open the large, beautiful box that held the taffeta gown that the Queen would have had made for me, the one with the delicate lace around the neck. I would put it on and appraise myself in my gilded mirror, amusing myself by flicking through an old book while awaiting breakfast in my room. At midday, the longcase clock would chime a twelfth time and then the soft click of the wheels and hooves of a brougham, sent by the Queen, would follow, coming to a discreet but firm stop outside the Schoens' front door.

I can picture Forbes' face as if I were telling him this aloud. He would always indulge me, finding my high-minded expectations perfectly reasonable. He would stare into my face as if I were the most important person in the world, even back on the ship as we lurched through uncertain seas. He kept his balance and his calm, and I would watch my own fears melt away as he probed with thoughtful questions at the gobbledegook I spoke.

Perhaps I'm speaking gobbledegook again today but, just as he indulged me then, I shall indulge myself now and proceed to get this off my chest. It really is quite something to have a birthday – a day of special treatment, a day to be spoiled and adored – turn into an embarrassing and sad series of unfortunate events. Bad days are one thing, but how much worse they are when one is quite unprepared for them. Is it any wonder that I dislike surprises?

So, we have the birthday as I thought it might go. I shall now endeavour to explain how it in truth unfolded. Elizabeth, whom I will not call 'Mother' in this diary (it is enraging enough to push the word off my tongue when she stands in front of my face!), came up to my room soon after I awoke. She gave her standard little knock and her *always audible* little sigh, which she barely bothers to hide. She hates that I have her room. The master bedroom sits at the top of the rectory and it's the largest and prettiest of the rooms here. Of course, that isn't saying much in a house like this, pinned untidily as it is to the church next door.

Elizabeth must sigh before she enters and sigh again once she is in the room. She must walk in with the sweetest smile on her face and then glance round like a tortured martyr, steeling herself with a deep breath before saying whatever she wishes to say. Perhaps she is waiting for me to give up the room. I shall not; let me say that now. I am a young woman with few things; my belongings I guard jealously, as they say. The Queen had the chaise that sits by the window crafted the moment my return was confirmed. The lace curtains were donated from her daughter's playroom. The commode was made especially for me. The walls are painted the exact shade of blue I asked for after I spied it in one of the Queen's rooms. The Queen's painter redid the walls himself.

I am tempted to suggest Elizabeth can take her room, but she cannot keep the furniture and we will paint over the walls. I daresay that shan't go down too well. But the performance of her sighing affects me in rather an unpleasant way. She has this breathy voice, and I cannot quite say why I dislike it.

In any case, she opened the door and in she came. Before she stepped much further, her hand was already at her bosom and heaving with some misplaced, but most certainly *deep*, emotion. "*Sally*," she said, in that strange, soft tone, and I nodded and rose from the bed, lest she wander over and impose. I usually keep the curtains around the four-poster closed, but I kept them open last night so that the sun could stream in. Already, she made me regret the choice, and I made myself at home on the chaise before she could ask, "May I sit down?" as she always does if it is unoccupied, her eyes fixed on it.

I sat quickly to avoid her raising the question and she just said "*Sally*" again. I have made it clear that the Queen's pet name for me is between herself and me, but Elizabeth always feels the need to intrude. These abbreviated names are rather common in Her Majesty's household and among those at court, but it seems unusual in a sober reverend and his wife. Nevertheless, Elizabeth seems keen to adopt any minor habit she gleans from my relationship with the Queen. I even caught the Reverend calling her "Isobel" once with a bemused look, and I have no doubt that he had never done it before.

I will spare us all the speech that followed. Really, I do not dislike her, but she can be such a windbag at times. In any case, she stood before me, a cascade of words pouring forth with no apparent end in sight, when I realized she held in her hand – the very one pressed all the while to her bosom – some item. She saw my eyes dart towards it and felt it prudent to wrap up her pronouncements and reveal what it was she held. Going forward, I might fix my glance on some spare accessory she may be wearing just to bring her endless speech more hurriedly to a close. I suspect she envies the Reverend the sermons he gets to deliver on a Sunday. I cannot say I blame her; his life is certainly more interesting than hers. She held the gift out and, as I received it, she stepped forward to embrace me. I rather wish I had some rejoinder that might keep her back when she did that. I shall ask the Queen to share the reason why nobody at court embraces – yes, even the family – while everybody in the Reverend's church seems keen to. I shall insist, truthfully or otherwise, that restraint is a courtly virtue. She will never attempt to touch me again.

At the time I had little choice but to endure the embrace, although I attempted to protest, albeit feebly, that we were both about to collapse onto the chaise. She left soon after that and I think her eyes were actually wet with emotion. As to why, I could not tell you. My own eyes were dry and clear, but I felt a little unsteady. As I looked at the little package in my hand and opened it up to discover its contents, I felt the ground shift beneath me. I confess that when I say I dislike surprises, it is not from the standpoint of the opinionated young lady articulating a preference. It is rather in the voice of the disorientated child, transported once more to fearful worlds of an uncertain past, a hot and muggy daze in which life was a constant swirl of unpredictability. A small gift – a diary, a notebook – should hardly evoke such a response. But I found myself wondering, with a panic that grew into outrage, at which point Elizabeth decided this was right for me. I paced the room, tracing prior conversations to see what word I had let slip, which word she felt important enough to quietly tuck away in the reservoir of her memories and act upon much later. Ah! Yes. I had forgotten that I had expressed an ardent, if idle, love of memoirs and diaries. It must have been one of our more pleasant conversations.

She had been in my room – or rather *her old room* – sitting on the chaise longue, her hands tenderly stroking the fabric, and had begun to talk to me about this and that. Because she usually remembers that I loathe surprises she had begun with a frank admission.

"There is a girl that looks like you, one village over, who cleans the rectory there."

Always the opening line to a great conversation. What followed, that I can recall, were her fumbling attempts to get close to me through the medium of some washerwoman who was also African.

We stumbled haplessly through the conversation of inadvertent offences. She admitted to projecting ideas onto me because questions were hard to ask. She must have said *something*, mused aloud about whether I wished to express myself in my own words somehow.

"Well, these newspapers that print about you all the time ... could they not hear from you too?"

And that's when it happened. I said it. I said the words. I said, "*Something more personal would be ideal.*"

And like a serpent she took my words about honouring my voice and used them to create a *gift* for me that offended my character. My character, my being, my very self feels most empowered when I am prepared. I am destabilized by surprises. To give me a gift that is meant to empower me, delivered by a means (a surprise!) that I find disorienting and disempowering by design, is about the most manipulative thing one could do. Even if she does not know *why* I need to feel prepared all the time, she knows that I do. It is the little I can hold on to as my own. And she sabotaged that, in order to give me a gift!

I was left thinking thoughts like this, on my own, in my room, pacing in a little circle, fruitlessly, for what felt like hours. It had been hours; the longcase clock started to chime twelve and I had yet to put on my dress and jewels for my tea with the Queen. I could not hear the brougham and felt a sharp jab of relief as I rushed to put my outfit on. I scrambled into the lovingly chosen dress in haste; the jewels were not in the top drawer of the commode as I had expected. It is rare that I cannot find things, but occasionally I ... how can I put this?

I would say I lose time. It is only when something unexpected happens and, even if it looks, from the outside, rather benign, I am affected just the same. I find my heart racing, my feet taking swift and circular steps and then suddenly it is eve where prior it was midday. It is not something I mention at all, really, although they noticed it in Sierra Leone. The girls were ... well, they were girls. African or British, girls can be cruel, and when one is African, fêted like a Briton, and the other Africans are made painfully aware of this, then they behave as girls everywhere do. They gather together and subject the girl who stands out to ridicule. Rather than feel resentful of her supposed power they diminish it with their mockery. I could manage that, of course: have I not escaped the jaws of death with my sense of self intact? What could a cohort of girls, as orphaned as I, reduce me with? Almost nothing, until they spied that peculiar thing, the time I would lose, my forgetfulness. And no, I did not tell the Queen.

The first I told her about their treatment of me, about how unbearable it made my time there, what did she say? *"Tout cela, ce n'est pas la mer à boire!"* Which is to say, 'this is hardly much of an issue'. Dismissals are always more painful in French. That was all she ever said about it. But she was correct. I grew resilient and never raised a complaint again. When I wrote to her requesting I return, she did not hesitate. She knew I was not a whimpering child; I had the fortitude to withstand most unconscionable behaviour. So she did not ask me what happened or why, and I did not tell her. And no, I shall not be divulging it here, either. It is not an unvarnished thought, merely a historical fact. There is no virtue in reliving such moments.

Ce n'est pas la mer à *boire.*

So midday crept up on me but the brougham did not. It neither arrived by stealth nor with fanfare; it simply did not arrive at all. For Elizabeth, few days are quite complete until she has delivered me a lesson in piety, and my birthday proved no different. When the clock struck two, she reappeared in my room, hands clasped to her chest. "The brougham has yet to arrive?" she asked. It was a question that could only be rhetorical and said in that soothing voice that she offers her youngest children when they are red-faced and ill-tempered.

"It appears to have been delayed," I replied. By *two hours*? Neither of us believed that. But I needed no soothing. I was calm.

"Yes," Elizabeth replied quietly.

"It is not unheard of. Appointments can be missed." I stepped back from the window and walked over to the painted commode. "It was her gift to me last year. It was carved and painted just for me."

Elizabeth smiled. She was happy.

I was trying to tell her I was fine. I doubt that is what she heard. Or, if I may be so bold, even what she wanted. She never usually spoke so little. I confess I gabbled rather a lot.

"I could not presume to be dismayed by the events of today. Or the lack thereof, as it were. I am fortunate to have a monarch who cares quite so much for me. It is rather a blessing." I think I repeated that a few times. My hands were sweating; my chest felt slippery.

She kept up the placidity. Her face did not flicker.

"You are allowed to feel displeasure, *Sally*," Elizabeth said. Not, I suspect, at her calling me Sally.

Did I resent her pity? No, I resented her presumptuousness. Her superiority. I would have preferred to be left alone. "Why would I feel displeasure? Do birthdays not recur each year? Did the Queen make an appearance on *your* birthday?"

I remember her forehead creasing for the briefest of moments. "No, Sarah." Her tone was unchanged, but my proper name made a sudden reappearance. "*I* was not so fortunate."

"But you are hardly *unfortunate*," I said, or words to that effect. I reminded her that she surely enjoyed pleasant birthdays with loving family, without the need for there to be royalty present.

She took this to be a reference to her last birthday and chose to inform me of how joyless it has been. "Sarah," Elizabeth sighed, and her voice grew sombre. I needed to know that it was an "unfathom-able" gift, in fact, to have the Queen of England, of the British Empire, appoint herself to be one's protector, to care for me as she does. Yes, unfathomable apparently. As she, Elizabeth, did not celebrate her birthday last year. In fact, rarely does Elizabeth celebrate it at all. She helpfully informed me, lest I forget, that she had *seven children* to feed and care for, as well as meeting the needs of her husband, *and mine too*, all of which she was "deeply grateful for, having been so truly blessed by our Father". Although not blessed enough to get a single day in a given year to acknowledge herself, alas. By comparison – not that she would ever *compare* – "the affection and the patronage of an English monarch is an extremely rare gift," and she could not resist pointing out the rarity of said gift for "an African orphan". I was encouraged to reflect on this, and on the fact that I may be the first and only person in such circumstances to have attracted such favour. She cautioned me not to treat it so lightly.

"Well said, *Mrs Schoen*."

Elizabeth flinched.

"We should not take our gifts so lightly; you are indeed correct. I have a queen." The words hung in the air for a moment. Then, I added, "You have a family. Neither of us has what the other does. I cannot conceive of what a birthday might resemble, might *feel* like, were I surrounded by my family. By people who did not think my African-ness might make me unworthy of their affection—"

"Sarah, I did not at any point say—"

"Alas, today it appears I have neither queen nor family and thus perhaps, with regards to gratitude, your exhortations are somewhat misplaced."

She looked at me, as though trying to hide the extent of her annoyance. For once, in her petty pride, she seemed human. And in the silence that followed, as she looked at the floor, I found myself gritting my teeth and then saying, in something of a rush, "That was impertinent."

Elizabeth looked up.

"Of me. It was impertinent of me." Upon reflection, I do not think it was.

She stared for a moment, then smiled. "It is your birthday today."

Truth be told, I could behave like this every day.

She knew this too. It was difficult for the Schoens, and perhaps I should have had some empathy for them. They could not critique and report misbehaviour to the court. The Queen may not want to hear critiques from me, but she shan't hear them *about* me either.

Did this ever become a concern for Captain and Mrs Forbes? I suspect not; my memories of that time are so fond, perhaps a year was too brief for conflict to arise. But, of course, I am the Schoens' social superior. They are not wealthy naval captains, commanding their own ships and owning beautiful land. Unlike the Forbeses, the Schoens do not have a carriage of their own, nor do they usually accompany me to Windsor Castle when I visit the Queen. The Schoens would not be visiting the castle today or any day at all were I not in their care. Fresh from Sierra Leone, from that school, with those girls, I was so relieved to be close to the Queen that I would have lived almost anywhere. But when I think of my life with Captain and Mrs Forbes, I remember our beautiful home. It is slightly surreal how comfortable I feel even saying it was *ours*. I do not know how much Elizabeth and the Schoens knew of them, or even how much the Queen knew of my bond with them. Perhaps she might have tried to reunite me with Mrs Forbes at least, rather than expecting me to start over again, with only a surname as my link to their legacy.

"It is your *birthday* today," Elizabeth repeated.

"It is," I replied, a little perplexed at the re-emphasis.

Elizabeth's eyes lit up. "I think this permits some *unorthodox* behaviour."

"What does that mean, precisely?"

"It means ... that if the carriage has not come to collect Sally, then perhaps, as Mr Francis Bacon is wont to suggest, *Mahomet will go to the mountain*."

"You are suggesting that..."

"If the castle will not come to her, Sally should go to the castle."

7 September 1860
The Rectory, Palm Cottage
Gillingham, England

Forgive me, I fell asleep. Writing one's story is all very noble, but in truth it requires extended time alone, which is all but impossible in the day. But then by nightfall, one writes, one reads what one has written ... one falls asleep. So the seventeenth birthday of Sarah Forbes Bonetta may require two, perhaps even three entries to complete. Such is life.

Where were we? Ah yes, Her Majesty Queen Victoria had forgotten to send a carriage to bring me to tea at the castle and Elizabeth was daring me to march over there myself.

I was surprised. "I should go to Windsor?" I asked. "Is that what you mean?"

"Well, we shall come with you."

"We?"

"The Reverend and I."

"You shall join me for tea with the Queen?" And before you ask, I was not opposed. At the time I thought it would have been quite a sweet suggestion. Elizabeth went out of the way to insist this was not the case.

"We would not impose on your time with Her Majesty, Sarah. We do not intend to enter the palace! We shall accompany you on the journey, is all."

Heaven forbid a girl might want *three* people gathered in her honour for birthday tea.

I nodded, trying to keep my face blank. "Ah."

"You are a young woman of noble birth; you should not travel without some kind of chaperone at your side."

"Ah." Yes, again.

"To others this could be deemed an impetuous decision. Birthday or not, the Queen's courtiers shall be less forgiving than Her Majesty. Our presence will—"

"Legitimize my behaviour?"

"Well..." Elizabeth smiled. We both did.

"I shall wait downstairs. Fetch a coat." Elizabeth said, walking to the bedroom door.

"Why?"

"We are not travelling in a brougham, Sally. We are taking a train, and we cannot have you staining your dress. I shall fetch the Reverend." And with that she slipped out of the door. I stood staring after her; perhaps it was my birthday after all.

The journey there was tense. The Queen had always been a little bold, a touch daring, but as we boarded the train, I realized that I did not know how she would feel about us turning up like this. The unpleasantness of the train, humid and packed tight with unwashed people, was compounded by this new anxiety. James marched through undeterred, while Elizabeth and I struggled behind him. What began as a daring idea in my bedroom started to unravel as the train chugged along to the castle. With every body that pressed against mine as we sought empty seats, and each face that caught my eye with a hostile unending stare, this fantastical plan grew more silly, my mood more sober. I would have taken any available seats just to put an end to the staring and give my poor beleaguered legs a rest, but it was not to be. James would stride past any single empty seat, as though the birthday girl's needs were not a priority. I finally spotted an unoccupied row, which he had inexplicably strode by. As I called out to him, "Father..." and caught an uptick in curious gazes, I added, "*James*," and he turned to me in mild surprise. This, of course, is why with the Forbeses I only travelled in a carriage.

"There is a row, here," I said, speaking as quietly as I could, hoping he could just read my lips. The row of seats was weathered. The fabric might once have been green. Damp and mottled, the seats looked like they had had a previous life, abandoned outdoors in an overgrown garden. Neither he nor Elizabeth would have expected me to sit there, certainly not without complaint. And not on my birthday. But seats were scarce and people were plenty – and the journey was long. I can inwardly grit my teeth with the best of them and maintain a placid

19

face if I choose. Did I not endure however many cold wet nights on HMS *Bonetta*? I turned to Elizabeth with an emphatic nod and relished the look on her face. So proud. I wanted to laugh. Her endless desire to humble me appeared to be bearing fruit, it seemed.

James was quiet for a moment, his face impassive.

"Sarah," he said, "I think you have forgotten which day it is and where we are going." I could not put an exact finger on his tone. It was the kind Forbes might have employed, had a child performed an impromptu dance at a funeral. "You are not sitting in third class. Obviously you shall be seated in the first-class carriage."

I felt a flush of relief, I cannot pretend, but it was swiftly followed by irritation. Why did we not simply enter first class on the platform? Why did we fight through the sweat and grime of working bodies in second and third? Perhaps he thought the first-class carriage was *de rigueur* to me and as such I would not appreciate the efforts they made on my behalf, unless I saw the horrors of second and third? I almost wish I had spoken, but I do not know what I might have said. *There was no need for the performance, Reverend. First class is quite as unfamiliar to me as it is to you. I rarely use any public form of travel. I travel privately; I am always sent a carriage.*

I did not say a word. I kept my composure and my silence as we went through the train. As we finally waded through the muggy carriages and pushed our way into first, I let out an involuntary sigh. James looked over his shoulder at me; his expression was smug.

A few hours later, as we disembarked at Windsor and proceeded to the Long Walk towards the George IV Gateway, I felt a sense of dread settle in my stomach. I had only ever travelled down the road to Windsor Castle by horse-drawn carriage, and the view from there was quite different. The walk was lined on both sides with identically spaced elm trees that gleamed an imperious green. Rolling down on wheels in a carriage sent by the Queen, there seemed something soft and benevolent in the vibrant row of endless trees that stretched the length of the walk. On foot, each step was a slap against the grit of the ground. I struggled to shake the stones from my shoes, and the unceasing stream of elms had the foreboding leer of a forest. I could hardly see the gateway up ahead and in truth I usually paid little attention. I would sit in the brougham unaccompanied, either reading a book or simply having a rest, as we rolled through the gateway and into the Upper Ward. For less formal visits there would be two courtiers waiting to take me from there to the Inner Hall, at which point another courtier would take over and escort me into whichever room the Queen had requested we meet.

As we traipsed down the unending walk, a sense of disquiet hovered over us all. James was still striding ahead without breaking a sweat. I tried to match his pace, if not his speed, and thus was still some way behind, sweat pouring down my face and soaking through my dress. Elizabeth was so far back that I could not hear her footsteps as she walked. I could, however, hear her tired gasps of pain as she struggled to reach us.

There were two guards standing by the George IV Gateway, and they looked from James, red-faced and sticky in his reverend's collar, to me, even sweatier, my taffeta dress hidden by a grubby overcoat Elizabeth had insisted I wear to keep the outfit clean. The four of us stood wordlessly for a moment and I closed my eyes, trying to catch my breath. In the end, James stepped forward to murmur some words to the guard standing closer to him, but before he had finished his sentence, the man scoffed aloud and said, "No. Do not be absurd."

Blame the endless journey, the long walk, the sticky train, the hours spent with this couple in awkward silence; in retrospect I do not quite know the reason, but I felt a flash of indignation. "I have an appointment with the Queen!" I snapped, and James turned to me, his eyes flickering for a moment. He looked ashamed. The guard looked sneeringly at me before turning to his companion. But the companion did not return the mocking glance. He looked down at his feet and then stared outwards, past them. Despite everything, I felt triumphant. "You remember me, do you not?"

He did not reply at first.

I knew then that it did not matter whether he replied or not. They would not let us in – this excursion had been for nothing.

"I am certain the Queen will take kindly to your behaviour this day," I announced with as much grandeur as I could manage, while cold sweat slithered down my neck. "Or rather, she shall if I ask her to."

Turning to leave, I nodded to James. "Come now, James," I added, and began to head back up the Long Walk. I could not hear him walking behind. In fact, there was silence beyond the echo of my own footsteps – until the guard called out to me.

"We did not get the order today. I cannot let you in because ... Miss Bonetta ... Sally!"

I stopped and turned around, raising an expectant brow.

The first guard turned to the second, his own brows having shot into his hair. "*Sally?* Surely that is not ..."

"The protégée of Her Majesty, Queen Victoria," the second guard said. "It is."

The first guard's eyes widened and he swallowed hard for a moment before returning to his earlier sneer. "She could be the Queen's *daughter*. She shall not be entering this castle tonight."

"On what grounds?" I demanded. "I have been here every summer for the past four years. It is my birthday."

"It is *at the Queen's discretion*. She has not chosen to invite you today, it appears. You cannot just arrive and expect to be seen."

"I did not! And I resent the false accusation—"

"Ah, you *resent* it, do you?" the first guard repeated, his mockery barely masking a layer of anger.

"I was promised a visit today—"

"Oh, you were *promised*, were you? Does Her Majesty answer to you, then? Or rather, does *your protector* answer to you?

Is this what you want to insist?"

My eyes widened. "You are being childish. I cannot fathom why. You have a role to play; why can you not play it? Escort me into the Inner Hall and send a courtier for the Queen. This is what has always been done—"

"Is it? A sweaty reverend comes to the castle with someone like you and demands a reception with the Queen? Is that how it is always done?"

Nobody said anything.

I was fine.

James was speechless. The second guard too. He looked at the first, his mouth turned down, awkwardness etched in every line.

I was fine.

Emboldened by the collective silence, the first guard continued. "Does she keep a *menagerie*? Are you coming to stay ... and be displayed?" He was smiling fully now, but I could still see a tight coil of rage just beneath the supposed amusement.

A menagerie. Well. I was *displayed* when I visited the Queen. She would have me sit in on diplomatic meetings with foreign leaders. I would arrive the evening prior and watch the military guard greeting their arrival. I would sit with the Queen and her international subject – or in some cases, royal equal – and after a brief introduction would be allowed to watch the discussions unfold. I was both a spectator and a spectacle.

The Queen had made it clear she wanted me to know that there were many upstanding Africans in the world and where possible I was to know them personally. She wanted me to be proud of my heritage, she said. She knew what village life with the Schoens might otherwise make me feel. But in this guard's mouth the gesture took on a new life of its own. I have been in newspapers before: the well-educated upper-class girl from "aristocratic Africa" as one article had written. What was "aristocratic Africa", precisely? "An important distinction and a reflection of your high-born status," the Queen had told me in decisive tones. Other articles erased that fine distinction:

Rescued from certain death at the hands of the 'brutes of Dahomey', whose kingship is unworthy of note, by none other than the Queen's own English naval captain, Sarah Forbes Bonetta was bestowed the highest honour a young girl could ever hope to earn. She held the patronage of a monarch, or to use Her Majesty's words, young Sally was the 'protégée of Queen Victoria'.

The Queen had grown tired of my critique by this point, but I had failed to see the compliment within. The King of Dahomey was rightly degraded, but in a manner that drew us together. It was insulting, erasing, and the first guard's little diatribe was more of the same.

It was not until later that I remembered James holding my hand, steering me round. I keep trying to recall how we got back to the train, at what point we met Elizabeth on the walk – but most of what followed was a blur. I have the memory of James's clammy hand and the sounds of shoes crunching the ground out of step with each other. A continuous, disjointed slapping and cracking of stones. But I cannot remember much else until we were seated back on the train, making our way back to the house.

It was almost dark when we arrived home. James unlocked the door and I strode through in silence, heading towards the stairs. There was a light cough from behind. I gritted my teeth and came to a stop. Elizabeth will have looked to James to insist he take the lead. Neither he nor I had much patience for this. I used to consider it a quality we shared. *"Family resemblance surpasses mere blood,"* after all. It was the Queen who had told me this, when I was a scared little child, spending one of the first nights away at Windsor Castle. *"You, dear Sally, are more like me than my very own girls,"* she had said, sitting beside me, on the edge of the bed. I was still new to England, and anxious to be spending a night without Forbes nearby. The Queen had put me at ease; she had known precisely what to do and say.

James could only stutter awkwardly as Elizabeth repeated her pointed cough. I felt a cry of frustration tangle silently in my throat. "S-S-Sarah, would you ... would you join your mother and I in the kitchen, please?" James said finally.

Mother. As a word it is neither ceremonial, nor frivolous. It is not an entitlement either, unless one actually gave birth to the person in question. It is an intimate word and, for those without mothers of their own, a private term, applied to patrons carefully selected. It was not until the first year came to a close that I began calling Mrs Forbes 'Mother', and within weeks I was being separated from her. Mrs Phipps felt very much *like* a mother to me; she was always so kind and effective at handling everything for me. Her husband is no longer the Queen's Keeper of the Privy Purse, but she still chooses to assist when she can. I have known her from the moment I stepped off that first ship. I do not call her 'Mother'. In my head it was only the Queen who was ever closest to really being a *living* mother to me. I thought she felt the same. She would not let people call her my patron; I was not her ward, or anything so formal and staid. 'I am your Protector,' she had always said, and once I asked her what the term truly meant. 'I consider it akin to a godmother. A protector does what a real mother should, or would, if she were able. She acts in her protégée's interests, she prepares her path, gives her good counsel, she helps her grow into a young woman. She protects her, she acts with care.' "As your protector" became her favourite way to start a conversation, or outline a request. We would both smile when she said it.

I have had my difficulties with this term, but now both feel pathetic. Protector. Mother. Every woman who grants me a smile is given a maternal title. It makes me seem desperate somehow.

It feels odious.

Elizabeth echoed James's request. "Please join us in the kitchen, Sally."

I turned to follow them.

It was rare in their household for any room that was not a bedroom to be empty for long. Every one of the Schoens' seven children was able to walk, and keen to run or try to, so the house was a constant swell of noise – except for my room, which, standing on the top floor of the house, a world away from the others, was an ocean of calm that the chaotic sound strained to reach.

Private conversations were therefore rarely conducted in the house. The Reverend would invite me to talk with him in the church instead, a distinction that sparked mutterings among his elder children, who felt aggrieved that they were not treated with the same care. But today it appeared that the children were still out and, given the nursemaid was also absent, it seemed clear they were out together.

James and Elizabeth stood around the deal table in the centre of the kitchen. Both pairs of eyes were fixed on me. I looked around the room. Glass and china stood unwashed in the wooden basin, plates were stacked on the table, instead of on the rack, soot from the chimney had gathered in the unused iron saucepans. Looking at it turned my stomach.

I sighed.

"You have every right—"

"Pride—"

They spoke at the same time. It was amusing. My mouth twitched.

Elizabeth ploughed on. "You are allowed to feel annoyed, upset, frustrated. They did not treat you as you deserved. It was demeaning! I feel demeaned."

I sighed. Politely, I said, "I really wish you would refrain from this incessant need of yours to grant me permission to feel. I am neither hiding nor holding in whatever emotions you think I am, nor do I require your authority to express them. I cannot help but note that, once more, you are being presumptuous. You might have asked me how I am and proceeded thus. You did not."

Elizabeth looked stricken. She always does. I was calm. I had spoken calmly, I felt calm, and I was unperturbed by her response. If I had to endure a sermon from James next, I could at least maintain outward composure and count backwards in my head until it came to a close. James glanced at Elizabeth and then at me. He pushed his spectacles over the bump on his nose and straightened up, as though preparing an inaugural lecture. "Pride has felled many great men, Sarah. Far greater men than—"

"You find me *proud*?" I snapped, composure forgotten.

"No, Sarah." James shook his head, his eyebrows raised for a fleeting moment. "I meant the courtiers at Windsor Castle."

"The courtiers?" I sneered. "Why even think of them in the sphere of 'great men'? They are *servants*."

"Well, they are not quite—"

"And they treated me like a *slave*."

"Oh, Sally, no!"

"No?" I repeated, the heat crawling up my cheeks. "No? But, *Mrs Schoen*, have you not been longing for me to reveal my feelings? Did you not want to hear these words? To have me speak about what it feels like to live in my skin. Did you not wish to sink your hands into my flesh and rummage around? To *know* of the experience, to absorb it yourself. The presumed pain, the presumed humiliation."

"Sally, you cannot say—"

"Sarah, it may be your birthday, but that is a little unkind."

"No, Reverend, I would disagree. What is *unkind* ... w-w-what is *unkind*..." I tried to speak; the walls began to swim. I took a deep breath, speaking quickly in case James interrupted. "An example of 'unkind behaviour' would be to watch someone endure the height of indignity, on the single day of the year that is meant to be theirs. To watch that indignity unfold in silence and then request that person relive that indignity once more, so that you can watch it happen again. To deny them the right to suffer in silence and then criticize the words they use to describe it. You wish to add to the humiliations of my day? I do not wish to endure that. So I shall retire to my room. But I do thank Mrs Schoen for the wisdom she imparted at noon when she told me to practise gratitude and humility. I have, but of course, much to be grateful for. How many lowly Africans have a queen as their protector? How many African girls have had the pleasure of watching their parents murdered in front of them, followed by their siblings? How many young girls are captives awaiting the same fate only to be 'rescued' and dragged across seas for months with no explanation? How many African girls are blessed to be ferried around like a travelling case from one ship to the next, one country to the next, at the whims of their lone consistent *self-appointed* guardian? How many orphaned girls live, as I do, so far away from their culture and their people, and their guardians are too busy to honour the promise of seeing them on their birthday? How fortunate I am; how fortunate for me that her courtiers, who have seen me visit every year, still spoke to me like I was..."

I did not finish. Three of the Schoen children stood frozen at the door.

Elizabeth was openly weeping. James's mouth was taut and his eyes downcast. Neither had spotted the children. I walked past them all. I ran up the stairs, into my room, pulling the door shut behind me. I stood in the centre of the room. I cannot recall for how long or what I thought about. But I was interrupted by a quick knock on the door. It was less a request for entry than an announcement of an arrival. Before I could answer, the door was open and the Reverend stood at the entrance.

"I..."

I hardly knew what to say. But I did not want to revisit the earlier conversation.

"Sarah Bonetta," he paused. "I do not have much information, but I have been waiting for the right moment to share what I do have with you. I have a smattering of facts that confirm one undeniable truth. You are not a *lowly* anything, you understand? Neither are you an aristocrat. You should know exactly who you are. Tonight I will tell you."

This time, the pause is rather more intentional. I am tired and it seems like a good moment to stop. There was no real suspense, of course. He simply told me what I did not already know. I am *inventing* a little break for mystery's sake, but really so I can conclude this entry, blow out my candle, get under my duvet and sleep soundly. The rest of this episode shall follow soon enough.

I shall tell it, perhaps tomorrow.

12 March 1861
On a train
Somewhere, Scotland

My apologies for the long silence. For those unused to diary-keeping, maintaining a consistent habit takes some time. Especially as I wanted to get that whole encounter down and, well, what followed was so overwhelming that I did not have the mental space.

Anyway, I have been granted the gift of alone time so many months on from my last entry and, while it feels odd to write while journeying, and odder still to be recounting a story from so long ago, it also feels like the best and only time. Expect liberties to have been taken with the details; I simply cannot claim to recall what took place almost a year ago, but I am actually glad I have the diary through which to try. That I have grown to feel grateful for this gift is its own surprise.

It was the night of my birthday and the Reverend had told me I was "not an aristocrat". I remember him standing at the door, looking at me, waiting for me to invite him in, to wash his sins away. For a bitter moment, I wondered whether, were an ardent young man to have turned up outside my door at this time and claimed to have some factual information to dispense, he would be granted the benefit of the doubt? Or was the Reverend's collar supposed to exempt him? He was not wearing it then.

"Come in, Father," I said, stepping back as I did so.

He entered without looking at me, his eyes on the ground. "You are not an aristocrat."

"You mentioned this, when you first knocked." I paused.

"I mentioned what you are not." The Reverend took a deep and sober breath. "I did not tell you what you are."

What am I? A barnyard fowl? Or is the African officially some non-human species?

"Tell me ... *what* I am," I echoed. Was I bemused or insulted? Or both?

He frowned and shook his head. He blushed. He could not seem to stop blushing. He shook his head harder but went redder still. I wanted to remind him the blush came from within; it would not fall from his face if he shook it hard enough. "Who," he said, his eyes trained on his shoes. "*Who* you are."

"Who...?" I faltered. Then I straightened my shoulders and looked over his head. "Reverend James, let us set aside the suspense. Please be forthright and matter of fact, as your sermons so often are."

Relieved, he nodded in agreement, but his skin was still crimson, his mouth pinched tight. "Yes ... well, Sarah is not the name you were given by your parents."

I tried not to roll my eyes.

He may have sensed it, for then he spat out, all in a rush: "Sarah, your name is less important than your status. Though your name has changed, your status remains. You are not an aristocrat. An aristocrat is born to a noble family. You were born into royalty. You are a princess. Your family were not just from the Egbado clan; your parents were the Egbado king and queen." I remember struggling to follow as the Reverend continued recounting my own history, of which I had known, until that moment, painfully little. "Your parents were monarchs and they ruled their territory well; it was a safe haven for those fleeing slave hunters. The Dahomey kingdom was at war with the Oyo Empire. The empire fell, fractured ... and the Egbado terrain was formerly a part of it. The Dahomey king, King Ghezo, was a rival. But as a small state without an empire behind it, your parents' kingdom was always under threat. King Ghezo was killing all remaining royalty from the Oyo Empire. As a result..."

I tried to take it all in. It was not unlike trying to recognize a distant strain of familiar music. The Reverend continued talking; I kept waiting for ... something that even hindsight cannot answer. Some inner affirmation? An inexplicable but authoritative click of memory lurking somewhere in my bosom?

"Wait."

I wanted to put the pieces together. My parents' kingdom was once part of the Oyo Empire. They left the Oyo Empire and created a kingdom of their own, with no empire and without subjugating anyone. It was called the Egbado kingdom and it was a small state. The king of the Dahomey kingdom, a much larger state, was destroying the Oyo Empire and killing all its royalty, including those dwelling beyond. He killed all my family. Happy birthday, princess!

The Reverend stopped abruptly. "Please." He gestured to me and then to the room as though inviting me to sit and enquire.

I ignored this. "I am not an aristocrat."

"Yes, well—"

"Because I am ... *higher* than aristocracy?"

"Correct."

"I am royalty?" I confirmed.

"You are a princess. An Egbado princess."

I swallowed.

"Y-your ... I was given access to Captain Forbes' notes from when he first rescued you," he said quickly.

My stomach shivered at the prospect of another surprise.

"You were born in Abeokuta, Egbado. Your name was Aina. Omo'ba Aina. In Yoruba, *'Oba'* is used as queen, or king; 'regnant' is used here. And the word *'Omo'ba'* is 'child of the monarch'."

"Omo'ba qua Princess?"

"Yes. Aina, not Sarah or Sally."

"So I am not..." *Not inferior to anyone. I am the child of monarchs; not even Queen Victoria was that! I am a princess!*

"Well," the Reverend spoke as though he could divine my thoughts. "You should remember something else too. Yes, you are royalty, but your lineage is much greater than the titles of man. Your parents left the protection of an empire to command and protect a small kingdom where people did not have to be enslaved. Titles do not have to matter. Your family had titles, but they preferred the honour of opposing slavery – before even the British Empire took the lead in abolition – to secure others from cruel rulers of power. You are a princess, yes. But you know many princesses, you are both daughter and protégée to queens. *This*, your family's legacy as protectors of slaves – who lost their lives to that legacy – this is a lineage money cannot purchase, pride cannot equate, land and rank can never surpass. Very few have it: the opportunity to wield power and the wisdom to choose humility. You must cherish this, above all else, as the gift your ancestors bequeathed you."

Is it really? I held my tongue.

Only the Reverend could take a revelation that should embolden me and use it as a weapon to hold me down.

The world may think you are a mere African, but you are in fact a princess. However, you must act like you are lower than an African, because your parents did, as rulers, and were killed for it, and wanted you to have that wisdom. To subjugate yourself so others may then kill you.

What a charming analysis!

So. Forgotten by the Queen, spurned by her servants, informed by the Reverend that I am as royal as Her Majesty's children and, as the child of a monarch, more royal than the Queen herself, perhaps.

And I received a new name. My old name. My first name. My real name.

Aina.

Princess Aina.

Omo'ba Aina.

Why did Forbes not tell me this?

Why rename me Sarah, of all things? *Sally* following that? Why could I not keep *Aina*?

Princess Aina Bonetta of Abeokuta.

Yes. It fits, would you not agree?

There is a ... a prosody to it, a rhythm the silly Reverend cannot muster in any one of his sermons.

I shan't erase entirely the names that followed, though. I am still Bonetta. But not of Her Majesty, ship or no. I belong somewhere: to and of Abeokuta, then and now.

I should know by now such moments do not last.

I am referring to my previous entry, but also to the moment I find myself in right now. This unused sitting room is a forgotten place in the Queen's apartments that she used to let me play in as a child when she was taking private appointments. I slipped in to see whether it might be as empty as it used to be, and for now it is.

Such moments of reprieve are usually curtailed by one person in particular. At least, when it's intentional.

Annie pushed me, on purpose, when I descended at noon the day after my birthday and the Reverand's revelation. It is not a day I shall forget, even if I have to recount it one hundred years from now. You will soon enough see why.

Typical Annie. I let my distaste for her conduct be known.

"How could I push you? You are behind me." Her voice was cool; it held a light sneer.

Ah, so she has a touch of cowardice, deep within her breast. Am I surprised?

"You moved backwards, into me!" I marched in front of her to demonstrate. Annie stepped sideways; she was not so keen. Bullies rarely are.

She had caught me on the bottom stair. I had stumbled back, but as she strolled away, I stalked after her, forcing her to halt. My tone was accusatory – and I was none too quiet about it.

"First it was a push. Now a 'move' backward?" A smile – small, malevolent. "Goodness. A couple of new names and you start to forget everything."

A couple of new... So the Reverend had gone and told the whole family, had he? But of course. My tragedies, my triumphs, all just fodder for their breakfast conversations. "How dare you!" I hissed.

"How dare I?"

"Yes!"

"Did you not falsely accuse me?"

"A semantic distinction!"

"Ooh, *semantic*!" Her eyes lit up. "So there are some definitions you still recall?"

"Of the many you have never learned?"

Her face hardened.

Yes, Annie. I can be mocking too.

"Shall I call you 'Princess', then?" She hitched the smug look back onto her face. I had seen it before, on that servant of the Queen. The outrage, bitterness, attempted superiority.

Should you be talking to me at all? I did not speak the words, but my eyes did. Does telepathy really exist, I wonder? And can such connections be built upon mutual dislike? For she read my words as one who heard them aloud.

"The title," I straightened my shoulders, "is 'Omo'ba, child of the monarch'."

Her eyes widened, performing shock. I knew what she was about to say: *I do not care—*

I spoke over her. "You *should* wait to speak." My tone was innocent. "I was not finished. Omo'ba means 'child of the monarch'. Anyone can be a princess or even a monarch. One can marry into it, or have the mantle passed from kin to kin in search of a suitable heir... Well, I shall not bore you with details you shan't ever have *any possible* use for. Few are direct descendants. Queen Victoria is the first child of the fourth child of the prior king. I am a direct heir. Not unlike yourself! To the ... clergy. It is also ... uncommon, I am certain."

Annie flushed. "Oh, are you?" she snapped.

"Well, I have not granted it much thought. You must have devoted hours to it."

"So you are *this* person."

"*This?*" My voice dropped low. "Do not be shy with your

categorization, clergyman's daughter. What *type* of person do you believe me to be?"

"No, who do you believe yourself to be? Superior because you have dead royals as a family?"

"Superior because I do not push or bump or touch people to convey my displeasure and then, like a coward, evade the consequences."

"I did not push you. You just cannot walk."

"Yes. I cannot walk. This sounds quite plausible, Annie."

"Ooh, *plausible*. You think your advanced vocabulary is impressive? You are as petty as the children."

"You say, having pushed me and started a row to avoid confessing to it! Child of a clergyman, indeed."

"What is so wrong with the clergy?" she began hotly. "You are content to live in our house!"

"I would not say content..."

"Then leave! You have not been requested. You were placed with us! If you are superior to our village rectory then, please, be gone! I am sure the air and the sky shall furnish your princesshood, princess-ship, your *Ooombooba* royalty. Your status will feed you!"

"Well, if you think this is charity, that your parents took me in because I was a princess, then the idea you elect to ridicule is rather a plausible one."

Annie blinked. *Surprised? You thought this was not a transactional arrangement. Ooh, Annie, you have much to learn.* I did not say this. Do not ask why. Perhaps I wished to spare her parents my ire. Or perhaps this was rather too easy a remark to make. One saves their efforts for a worthy adversary. Annie was many things; this was not one of them.

It grew ever more bitter. Some words escape me, but I recall her threats got rather physical.

"I shall drag you from here and out into the village. How much of a princess are you, when publicly rejected?"

Rejected? By a village of the illiterate? By the child of man of the cloth on a stipend? How much did their opinions matter? I kept quiet but rolled my eyes.

She read my thoughts on my face. The revulsion curled on her lip. I knew what was coming. She straightened her shoulders. "Tell me, can a princess also be like you"

I swallowed hard. Did it sting? Tell me, when in pain, how much of it lies in the surprise? I was waiting for this.

"Can they?" My face was blank, but Annie kept going. Like a bloodhound who smelled fresh meat, she knew I was not as composed, inwardly, as my coolness implied. "I daresay, Sarah, African Princess, *pretender*, as the daughter of a clergyman I have access to a large number of collars. Do you suppose, were we to thrust you from this home – this humble home you think yourself above – and abandon you, dirty, orphaned, without living lineage or a parent to prove you are anything that you say ... and were I to place a reverend's collar on you, you might be sold in chains like all the rest? Like all the rest of the... If I cut you, would you bleed, just as they do?"

I was smiling before she finished. Her eyes narrowed. She had, no doubt, exhausted her repository of vengeful phrases. But goodness, I become an adult and those who I rank far above start slighting me with racial slurs every time I turn around? Would Elizabeth say it next? What was the purpose of the status if it subjected you to this nonsense?

"Annie, really. That was ... *quite* some imagery. I shan't forget a single word of it. It will make a compelling tale to recount in the future. I am sure whomever is listening, they will be struck by your narrative. Is this what Father James taught you to think about his collars?"

Her eyes had widened before I had even finished speaking, and her mouth dropped open; she tried to retaliate but faltered, making inchoate sounds.

Should I have stopped? I did not.

"I would suggest a future career in writing. For a moment, it seemed you had an aptitude for it – but really I am confusing appetite with aptitude. And there have been a few confused conversations today. Aptitude in the sphere of the arts would include a knowledge of language – several languages, even – but we can settle for the one you were raised to speak. And thus begin our *corrections*. 'Pretender' is not the pejorative you believe it to be."

I smiled. I could afford to. "A pretender is not a literal interpretation of 'pretend' in noun form. No, pretender comes from the French, '*prétendre*', and thus also the Latin, '*praetendo*'. And, well, I could elaborate but I think brevity has some virtue too. Thus, I shall say this speech deserves some fine-tuning, and what better way than with additional study? I suggest you consult your father's library, or simply tell him what word you are looking to understand. Typical of a clergyman."

Annie's nostrils flared here and my smile widened too.

"He is an honest man and he will attend to your needs forthwith. My surprise at your dishonesty, given you are the daughter of a clergyman, was entirely due to the fact that I had hoped, expected even, that you might have inherited your father's natural honesty and grace."

Annie's face was a picture! Really, I wish I had captured it somehow. I was certainly not deft enough at art or printmaking or any such thing, but I would have loved a painting of her unhappy expression. There's a limit to the number of faces one can make after behaving so poorly, especially when you answer with kindness.

She started to speak. Was that panic in her eyes?

It was I who was the bloodhound then. We were both adept at detecting the scent of vulnerability in the air.

I raised my hand to bring her to a silence. "As to your insistence on my exit – well, Annie, dear Annie, I hear you. Reluctant, I may have been; now I feel differently. I should leave. I shall. It may be best. You are correct. I am certain the loss of remuneration that your parents receive from the Queen of the British Empire for housing her royal ward will not make a dent in the finances of the Schoens. With the eight … or nine of you there are to feed. For now. Until you wed, and Frederick weds. I must confess, however, I have seen little inclination from either of you. But you are quite correct. The *favour* has been for me. Your parents have not benefited – they have suffered. What a travesty to endure: a monarch with an empire that stretches the whole world, but still has time to recall who you are, feed your family, parent your ward. Please convey my apologies."

I had not been looking at her; my hand pressed to my chest, I had spoken with the kind of sincerity best suited to eyes that are closed. And there are no entreaties that can be made with pleading eyes this way. *What might I say, were she to open her mouth and gibber with the same tongue that so giddily fantasized about putting a collar on me?*

"If I, alone, were to leave," I mused, turning towards her with concern, as a tiger with an overgrown snail lying between its paws, "I see such a move inviting quite some resistance. But I suspect my departure shall be met with smooth waters if I tell the Queen what the Schoens' eldest has been saying to me. I do also suspect that while having the Queen aware of your existence is a privilege, it is rather less of one if you become *mired in infamy*, courtesy of your dislike of her ward, because you insist she is a different *type*. Certainly if you engage in sordid fantasies about enslaving her. I am not certain the Queen will romanticize the idea of her ward being treated as a captive. I suspect we shall find out."

19 April 1861
Buckingham Palace
London, England

It does feel rather strange to be recounting events that took place so long ago. In my last entry, I was nursing the wound of Annie's comments, hoping to brandish it like a weapon, but in truth I did not tell the Queen what she had said. I still had my own grievances with the Queen that I did not wish to overlook and, while I never did find out the specifics of what was said, Annie clearly informed both the Reverend and Elizabeth about our argument. It was a fact I found irksome at the time but cannot recall why. Neither the Reverend nor Elizabeth broached the topic with me, but for what felt like months everyone in the household spoke to me with deference. I rather like that approach, or the idea of it at least.

In practice it was lonesome. Elizabeth would walk the house like one bearing the weight of a cross on their shoulders. Annie wore a perpetual moue, and nobody talked to me! The deference that I sought was from Her Majesty, and it appeared that her letters had tumbled into an abyss. Her memory of yours truly most certainly had, and life at the Schoens' became unbearable. The tiptoeing around was the worst. My mood would sour. For months on end I was irascible. It was always forgiven, but *too* easily. What fun is there in that? Not that my rages brought me any joy.

"Sally!" *Elizabeth. She dropped the piety, yes, but never the pet name.*

"Mrs Schoen?"

"You have a letter, Sally!"

I was amused at the relief in her voice, in denial about the relief in my own. We both knew what 'a letter' meant. Whom it must be from. We knew whose letters required announcements. It was in her right hand. Both of mine flew to it. I have never clenched anything so tightly. For once, she was silent and simply bobbed her head, opening her hand without flinching as I pulled the letter from it. I skimmed it and, as she took her leave, called out to her.

"Wait." My voice faltered.

She turned to look at me and for a moment her expression seemed bereft.

"No, it is not ... bad news," I said. But before her face could brighten, I added, "It is ... well, it is rather a short letter."

"Well Sally, Her Majesty is ... *Her Majesty*! She has so many demands on her time."

Am I a demand? I kept my lips pressed shut.

Elizabeth seemed to read my mind. For once. "When one is busy, one's favoured tasks are those they lose first, those they spend the least time on."

Nonsense.

"It is easier to disappoint oneself, to prohibit oneself from enjoying the fruits of life than it is to risk others being harmed by one's actions. I know this, Sally. I am no queen, but I have a house filled with children to whose needs I must attend. I have a husband whose calling before our Lord and Saviour is to be placed above my own. I must attend to him also. I must first and foremost be a pliant servant of the Lord."

And so her piety returned with the Queen's correspondence! I pushed it from my mind. I nodded at her as she continued, thinking about this upcoming visit. The Queen did not apologize or even acknowledge my birthday had passed, and the invitation was one of the shortest letters she had sent. But, having just endured a whole household of people avoiding me because of something their own daughter did, I was desperate and grateful for some warm, direct attention.

21 April 1861
The Rectory, Palm Cottage
Gillingham, England

How does one show they are disappointed with the Queen? It was a slow, wet day I was to sit through, waiting for a carriage. Did I doubt its arrival? It is not something to which I will confess. Elizabeth had clearly told Annie to say *something* to me, but it was unclear what or to what purpose. She hovered by my door when I opened it in the morning. I ignored her. I walked hurriedly down the staircase, but of course, the family was all gathered in the kitchen and painfully aware of the news. Elizabeth, looking with mild disappointment at my frock, shot a pointed stare just behind my ear.

Annie was behind me, I assumed, but the Reverend appeared instead. "Sarah," he said, and even his voice was bright. I began to wonder if their royal wages had fluttered off into the abyss as well, along with my letters. "You are excited for your trip today?"

"I shall be, should I hear the brougham arrive."

"It does not do to be impertinent," the Reverend said quickly, but he was looking at Elizabeth as he spoke, redirecting words to me as a puppet might.

He needed little encouragement to start a lecture unprompted, so my eyes darted between the two of them with some curiosity. I think Elizabeth feared what I may say next. Either way, she clearly saw something in my face that propelled her to candour.

I wondered for a moment if she would implore me not to report her precious Annie. Instead she said, "I am concerned at how little time you have left to dress. I do not think you intend to see the Queen dressed in this ... ensemble."

I wore an old white smock that someone had once donated to the rectory. I had borrowed it a year ago to wear while painting with watercolours. I did not paint often, and the smock was not besmirched. But it was not an outfit I had worn out anywhere before that I could recall.

"Yes, but what confirmation is there that I will in fact see the Queen today?"

"Sally..." Elizabeth's tone was cajoling; one might think I was at fault.

"It seems like a cumbersome exercise to dress *myself* with effort only for its intended audience to fail to show without warning. Had this not happened before, I might—"

The sound of hooves – the slippery skid of wheels cluttering to a panicked halt outside the rectory – cut through my words.

Elizabeth rose. "Go and put on your dress. Wear what you selected on your birthday and return here at once."

As Elizabeth ordered, I hurriedly replaced my informal smock with the dress I had planned to wear the last time.

I had been sent a *two-horse* brougham. Is it not endlessly amusing, how older people refuse to simply apologize outright? How they will always prefer to proffer you arbitrary jewels than grant the priceless gift of an apology – or their unfettered attention.

I cannot recall the first time I was summoned to the Queen in a special carriage. I wonder, having spent so many months swaying about on my namesake, the HMS *Bonetta*, whether the uneven gallop of a brougham – the sleek horses hastening forward, its large wheels sliding uneasily over hard, wet stones – would have left me as distressed that first time as it did today.

Did I really choose this for my birthday? The train, albeit entering in first class, would have been a smoother, more seamless choice. Two-horse broughams required both beasts to move in unison, together as one.

I sat back against the red velvet of this brougham, eyes closed. I could not envision the anticipation I had expected on my birthday. I sat, already seventeen, as I undoubtedly was then too, in a two-horse carriage, as she very well may have sent to mark the day then too. And while I had since experienced rejection, racism and what felt like months of loneliness, I still could not remember what had filled me with such anticipation.

Was it simply an hour of the Queen's attention?

The ground beneath the brougham shifted. The horses' smart gallop slowed into a light crunch. I could hear the stones shift to gravel beneath their hooves. I need not have looked to the window for confirmation; I knew we were finally on the Long Walk. But the heady, humid traipse that the Reverend and I had made with sweating faces and beleaguered bodies was a dream away from the journey today. I had no time to take more than a passing glance at the trees that lined the walk and wonder again at how they differed when viewed from this place – or quite frankly, this *pace* – before we were suddenly at the entrance, the carriage door was opened and I was gently invited to step out.

It felt different. I cannot quite say how or why; I just knew. I was escorted through the castle to her favourite meeting place, the Drawing Room, where every wall gleamed a sumptuous red. I was to wait for her, which was not unexpected, but it did leave me an inordinate amount of time with which to ruminate. Was there an additional painting? I saw nothing new. The gilded frames of the paintings clustered on the walls above her favourite seats still gave the room a medieval air. The ceiling was as gold and white as it always had been, the delicate pattern unfolding in an intricate but bold design that snaked its way around the top of the chandelier that hung in the centre. I had not looked quite so closely before, but it seemed unchanged to me.

She was late. I grew impatient, gripped with the feeling that she would disappoint me yet again – an indignity more insulting than her forgetting our birthday tea. I could imagine how it might unfold, how easily. Someone would be sent to talk to me, to escort me out, an apology whispered into my ear.

"Her Majesty has gone to Scotland, it would appear. Pressing matters have taken her from the castle. You are encouraged to return to the Schoens' home." All the while a cold sweat might trickle down my back. The guard at the entrance to the Long Walk would once more ... but I suddenly realized: the guards had changed. Neither man who had denied me entrance on my last visit had been there. How did I not notice as I entered today? I had little time to ponder what that meant, because the door was opened, she was announced and in my little, mighty *protector* came. I rose and sank into a courtesy. She looked impassive.

What was I expecting?

Affection? Embarrassment? I would have settled with acknowledgment, but little proved forthcoming. Her voice had a stretched quality to it. She sat opposite me, the small circular table an oasis between us. Serving staff pushed in glass tea trolleys, loading the table with cakes, sandwiches, tea, stacking the plates high enough to build a fortress. The table became a castle between us, and conversation struggled to breach its walls. Each word from the Queen had to be coaxed out, as if it cost her a great effort to speak.

"Sally," she said after a strained silence I could not think to fill. She stopped, looking at me over a cake stand. "I do recall ... why, your mastery as a seamstress." The words rang with relief. "I believe ... after Albert so fondly remarked on the slippers you made him, you told me you were crafting a pair for me. How goes your progress with this? Are you still sewing?"

Am I still sewing?

Your Majesty, I confess I quite forgot to bring the rich fruits of my labour, to proffer additional trinkets to garnish your castle. Were you intending to have me deliver your gifts on the day we gathered to celebrate my birth? Was that the primary exchange of gifts that would have taken place?

I did not say this. I did not say much.

"Sally?" The Queen lifted her china teacup to her lips in the ensuing silence. Her gaze met mine over the rim and I wondered what she saw in them.

I was not sure what I saw. The Queen I knew was fun. Warm. And on birthdays ... she was a little cheeky too.

"How is His Royal Highness?" I said finally, reaching for my own tea. The china felt so delicate against my fingers. The tea within was still piping hot and the fireplace was still blazing. She had not forgotten my loathing of the cold, of draughts, even as she continued to request that I visit her here, the coldest, most windswept of her homes, the castle filled with crumbling stone and listless ghosts.

Her hand trembled. She placed her cup with an inadvertent clatter onto the saucer. "He is quite well," she insisted in a high-pitched voice that told otherwise.

I sighed inwardly. Theirs was a marriage unlike any I had seen. How ironic that the British reserve, the Victorian culture of restraint, was helmed by a queen and her prince consort who seemed to burn with vibrant passions for each other. They were always so in love, even when they were caught in some temporary but heated feud, and I often wondered what that must be like – to be so vividly enmeshed but also able to speak so freely with each other. It was a love that was only possible by her superior status as queen. Were she the consort, would she not have to be meek and obedient to his whims?

Would I? Would I even one day be a queen myself?

I started and held my tongue. I could not ask. *I could not ask.* The reason was simple. All were gone. What is a queen with no palace, with only a mausoleum to honour her memory? Who can tell of your history from your audience of the dead?

"Your Majesty, I receive this news with gratitude. I always pray for his health."

It was her turn to jolt. Her eyes bulged for a moment. "He has always been sickly, my Albert. Too sharp a tongue – his continence could ne'er endure! He shall return to full health with speed. I tell you, Sally, this time is little different from those prior. We thank you for your prayers. It would have been so thoughtful of you to pay him a visit over the summer. He is so very fond of you; you must know that, Sally."

"I thought I would be paying you a visit, Your Majesty." The words rushed out, the tone hardly polite, but her eyes did not catch the flash of annoyance on my face. Her ears barely heard my remarks.

"Ah yes, we did have summer plans." The Queen looked at her teacup. The air between us felt leaden, morose somehow. "Should I have Alice join us?" she asked suddenly, in a brighter voice; her eyes did not move from their hold on the china.

"Princess Alice?" With every sentence came a new affront!

The Queen's daughters had long wanted to join our little gatherings and conversations. They, who could count on her being their mother, who would live forever in castles as princesses and even queens, would not grant me those moments I shared with her alone. My stays at the castle were always marked with the whiff of a female tantrum unfolding somewhere along a hall. Pleading voices and whimpers carried through gaps in the stone, sliding under the bedroom door, penetrating the walls. Prince Albert believed I would benefit from deep friendship with princesses.

I might have. But the Queen wanted our interactions to continue without their intrusion and I relished having her to myself. I relished being sought *by* myself, *for* myself, with no other addition bolstering the interaction.

"Yes, she has always wanted to join us," the Queen continued in her falsely bright voice. "You are so close in age, I think she may well be just what a young girl like you needs. You are going to have so much to talk about together very soon, after all!"

I barely took in her last line, filled as it was with foreboding.

"It is so good of you to encourage me to spend time with Her Royal Highness, Princess Alice, Your Majesty," I said with a sweetness in my voice. "One can never grow tired of family; the presence of one inspires the presence of more!"

She looked up at me, confused and yet incurious too.

I continued. "I think the opposite may be true as well. The loss of one inspires a search for others."

"Who has been lost? He is not lost!" the Queen suddenly snapped, a hand hard against her chest.

He? Albert? I could not fathom her odd behaviour today. "Who has been lost?" I echoed.

"Ah, Sally." Her chest seemed to slump. I was talking about my family, it seemed to say. *Again.*

"I was actually thinking about Captain Forbes."

"Oh?"

"The year I lived with the Forbeses is the first impression I had of what family life could look like. How it may feel, how its members are treated. And thus, without Forbes, without even his wife and their lovely children, I sometimes feel ... at sea. And of course, before we came to land, at sea is where we spent the majority of our time together. So to feel adrift is to think of Forbes, and to feel anchored means I think of them too."

The Queen was silent as I spoke. I realized she was waiting. Was there a question I might pose? She was not one to encourage idle complaints. Nor was I keen to give her a reason to correct me. Not today and not after everything that had led to this day.

"One thing I would like to ask of you, Your Majesty, is perhaps for any additional stories. Is there anything you could share with me about Forbes that you have not? Any gifts, even, that he might have left for me that I have not had access to? You are a mother; I am a daughter. I am a daughter looking to know more about her mother, her father. Or ... the closest I had to a mother and father that I can still remember. What would you want a daughter of yours to know, if you could not tell her yourself? Help..." I swallowed. "It may help Forbes to tell me what he is not able to share."

"Well, Sally, for Forbes you were something truly special. Where others are given trinkets and tokens, stories and memories, you, Sally, were given – as you do know – your *life*, by Forbes. You were granted your right to exist by this empire, by Her Majesty's Ship. It is why he named you for the ship, for *the* HMS *Bonetta*. It is why he presented you to me, after his arrival. The late Captain Forbes secured your rescue from the brute of Dahomey. A kingdom without honour or civilization, that could not recognize human beings for what they were, or children for their purity, instead of instruments of sacrifice.

And thus, Captain Forbes brought you to these civilized lands, where true monarchy resides, and placed you before me, as a gift. You did not receive tokens or trinkets. You are what *I received*. You are no token nor trinket, but you are the highest form of honour, a gift for a queen, that I might keep you from the brutes of the world untamed by my empire. You were promised safe haven here. That is what Captain Forbes gave to you, by delivering you into our arms, to be mine."

Was this adulthood at last? Did it require the placid smiles of repressed rage at increasingly insulting assessments? At the time it was all I could manage. Recounting such a tiresome speech now, the bones of which I had already heard, was altogether arduous enough. Need I reflect on how it made me feel just yet? It is late and the memory of it saps energy from my skin. Indeed I am grateful to be relaying these grim and unpleasant memories quite so many months after I had to endure them at all. It should hurt less, but actually it just hurts in a different way. Less immediate and sharp, but still slowly soul crushing.

25 April 1861
On a train
Heading north, England

I wanted to wait to write this entry until I could at least recreate the moment. And so I sit writing this on the train, about the extraordinary trip that I took to see the Forbeses in Scotland. I did feel proud of myself. I had handled those awful comments about being akin to a very nice brooch while maintaining my composure and I had been rewarded with something so wonderful I could hardly have dreamed of it happening. Perhaps this is what makes one an adult. Obedience for the sake of opportunity. As I received last month.

For it is not the case, I am certain, that the Queen, or Elizabeth Schoen, or whomever leans into their arrogance next, is entirely oblivious to the insults they dispense, or the dominance they attempt to vaunt as they do. They know what they say: they know its impact; they care about asserting whatever is thus implied and they *do not* care about how the other person feels. However, they are mindful that one may feel *something*, and it becomes a question of whether and how I choose to respond. As of late, I have challenged Elizabeth with an unfettered displeasure unbecoming of my heritage. Even upon learning of my elevated status, I sunk lower in the days following, verbally wrestling with Annie!

That thought was not allowed to settle without question. It is one thing to be proud of your high-born status, particularly in a land where all, including the lowborn, believe you to be inferior due to the shade of your skin. It is another to be seduced by superiority which puts some people directly above others. I cannot factor Annie's father's profession into my distaste for her, or my conduct. The daughter of a monarch should not ever be in a war of words. Even if she currently lacks the proper military force to go to war for her. But especially if her parents freed themselves from an empire to create a safe stretch of land for those who wished to live unyoked by others...

A rather more important point is that, much like the word Annie uses to describe me does not hold space for 'Princess Aina', 'vicar's child' reduces the great intellect of the dear Reverend and does not hold space for him! Pitiful though his performance at the pulpit may be, his is a rigorous and uncompromising mind, one that entertains my thoughts and ideas. When, since Forbes, was I given such grace? And back when dear Captain Forbes listened to my words, I had altogether too little of value to say. No, my wrangling with Annie was unbecoming of any such adult because she is callow and jejune.

Were she the daughter of the Queen, I would have lost the chance at leverage I gained over tea.

The Queen's merry narrative about my personhood – a princess born to a monarch flattened into an exotic jewel to be shipped overseas and worn as a brooch on the British monarch's fragrant bosom – was met with a gentle smile from my dear self. I allowed my lips to stretch as though flattered, my eyes low with a sadness that did not, *did not*, stem from the hubris of her comment, but from the obvious loneliness of this little jewel's journey.

"A jewel is such a rare and precious item."

"It is," the Queen replied, her own eyes slightly absent – I still wonder what preoccupied her that day. I suppose a fight with her husband, but in prior eras she might lightly reflect on them with me. I would, of course, agree with her and reframe his position as one that affirmed hers, and she would look appropriately pleased, her shoulders would drop a little, and following a deep breath she would briskly change the subject, a slight glimmer of affection dancing across her lips. But she was not inclined to share that day, and my interest in the problems of others, even *protectors* like my own, had waned for the moment. But her tone was keen to remind me that I should take the compliment and remain content.

And here I had to do some manoeuvring. One thing I shall always be grateful to Her Majesty for is that she does not indulge wallowing or endless oral complaining. Though she is a woman, she is a queen, and not a consort. It is a birthright but also a role, a responsibility, and she takes on such requirements with the minimum necessary emotionality. We may think of women as soft and naive, and the Queen is full of red-blooded emotion; however, endurance, resilience and practicality are the unspoken codes through which emotion must be tempered.

Therefore, if one is to risk a little pout or preoccupied self-reflection, it is wise to do so with a solution looming nearby. "To be seen as the jewel of a monarch, of a Queen, is a great gift and yet a lonesome one, I must confess." I straightened and looked her in the eye. Given her own preoccupations, I needed to be more direct and less meandering in my approach. "The Reverend divulged something he had withheld from me, on the day we celebrated – the day I was deemed to have 'come of age'."

"He divulged?" She looked at me, her gaze was piercing now.

Forgive me, Reverend, but you shall come to no harm. "He told me of my heritage, that I was *not* simply a woman of high birth in the town of my parents. They were the king and queen. I was the daughter of a monarch. With that revelation, I felt ... I felt alone."

"Alone?"

"Like that precious jewel. That which is rare is also isolated."

"Sally, tell me you are not isolated here." The Queen paused. Carefully, *it seemed*, she added, "Is it that you do not know anybody else who is a direct descendant of a monarch, myself included?"

"Princess Alice is the direct descendant of a monarch, Your Majesty," I replied. "And you, as the monarch, who is also mother to a princess, may well know more than I, how my own mother might have felt, were she able to see what became of my fate."

She did not speak for a moment. I could not read the expression in her eyes. I confess that there was a brief window of time in which this did not feel like a manoeuvre at all. I was being careful, yes, but within there was also candour.

I did not speak. I looked at the large square of untouched cake that grew dry on the table between us. When I raised my gaze to meet hers, her eyes were moist.

"A jewel is a great treasure, but it does not encapsulate the bond between a mother and a child." She stopped, her brow furrowed momentarily. I suspect she was remembering her own mother and the bond between them that held, by her own retelling, little affection.

Here, manoeuvring was again required. "It is between those who perceive themselves as mothers and are perceived as thus by their children."

"Yes!" Her voice was low, the emphasis clear. "You cannot recall your family, however. You could not speak to that bond."

The words, carelessly thrown, stung. I could see there was no malice; she was trying to make sense of my poetic narrative and she had a point. "No, I rely on *you* to speak to that from her perspective.

But I had that bond with the Forbeses. I believe that what makes people into a family is not necessarily determined by birth."

"That must be the case, dear Sally, given you are family to me. And why you must spend more time with Princess Alice. She too is the daughter of a monarch and will never be Queen – of the country of her birth. There are shared experiences that few without insight can hope to imagine, and therefore can never build bonds across. I understand that."

"It is how I felt with the Forbeses..." Boldly I added, "To have lost them was to have lost a second family. Well, I lost the Captain. We all did. And then..." I sipped my cold tea to give myself something to do with my hands.

The Queen did not speak for a while. I was not looking at her face. The room seemed still but for the china at my lips. My gaze dropped and I saw, in the stillness, she fidgeted with the jewellery on her right hand. "Mary Forbes is ... doing very well – she has returned to Scotland. She lives with the children in a castle of the clan. I was uncertain as to the virtues of maintaining that fondness between you both. You could not have joined her in Scotland, and certainly not as she tried to rebuild her family as a widow. Nor did I wish to cause pain to the next family who were to take you on, by letting you nurture a relationship elsewhere. Which is to say that Mary Forbes has oft inquired about you. There have been many letters..."

Many letters.

Many letters.

Many.

Letters.

MANY.

Many?

I overturned the table.

In my mind's eye.

In the real world, I looked into her eyes, filled with new insight but deliberately bereft of judgement. I need not bother; she would carry that herself. She might have been forgetful this year, but I had about a decade of evidence that she cared. I need only look saddened. The rest would fall upon her.

"Many letters?" I let the words hang for a moment. Then I withdrew my gaze and said, "Might she and I be reacquainted, Your Majesty?" My voice was *so gentle*. "In light of these new insights ... I find myself in need of, well, regular, frequent connection with ... family."

"Sally, you can always come here!"

Well, I tried, I did not say, but somehow the words appeared between us.

"The guards will be informed as to a more unofficial—"

"I should like to visit this Castle Forbes. I should like to see the children again."

And thus I found myself sitting tucked in a corner, in a first-class seat on an early morning passenger train heading out of the country. I was headed out of England, to the Forbeses' castle in Scotland. I have left the country before; I travelled to Freetown, Sierra Leone, and back again. And of course, I arrived here, one of my earliest solid memories, on that dark and surreal journey through nightmarish storms across several seas. So travel is not uncommon for me; I might say I am better acquainted with the breadth of the world and its far-flung reaches than even the Queen's children. However, I had never explored the countries within the United Kingdom that are outside of England. And I can state with confidence that there are few favourable accounts of Scotland that I have read.

Yet favourable it was.

Whatever I had read I think was, if little else, misleading. As such, the journey to the castle proved quite the delightful surprise. I was alone in my train car. Despite my racing heart, I looked out of the window more frequently than I would have expected. Would you not have assumed I might sit almost motionless, that I would ruminate on all that I could say or ask, on what she might look like now? On whatever was contained within those *many* letters? I did not know whether the children would be there, whether they would remember me, nor how she would feel about receiving me. There was so much I did not know, so much I was unaware that I did not know. But the train rumbled along nicely. For hours and hours across two countries. My eyes were turned to the landscape, unfolding outside. There were rolling hills. An endless parade of them, rising like the bosoms of gentle matrons, the kind one dreamed of but never found in Freetown. Soft enough to rest one's head against, albeit in brilliant, vibrant green. I had never seen such an expanse of nature – in this part of the world, that is. Freetown had more beaches than pasture, and we were not encouraged to explore either. The scenery in Scotland looked like little I had ever seen. Stretching quite so far. Mountains rising quite so high. Rolling hills, grazing livestock. It was not simply beautiful. To me, it was a thing of wonder. Scotland was a delight. I had not known what I was missing.

I was nervous to travel alone. I could not have taken a companion. The Schoens had not taken my trip at all well. Having them accompany me would not have helped matters. To them, I had been given a revelation and used it to distance myself from them. I had fled to a family that felt more sincere. It did not escape Elizabeth that the Forbes are a clan, Scottish nobility, and her breathy, emotive snapping oscillated between the Reverend and her favourite, Annie. It was clear she blamed him for the revelation and her for driving me further away. Whatever the problems I had had living among them before, whatever issues may have arisen between us before, I had not asked to travel to the Forbeses' castle. I heard their low whispers floating up the staircase at night.

"It was never about the Queen! Or her silence. Sally wanted to feel *seen*!"

"I suspect it was an issue with the Queen, but certainly her conflict with Annie did not help matters—"

"It took away her home. *We* took away—"

"Elizabeth..."

I think there had been sobs. It was not uncommon for Elizabeth to cry, but her tears increased in frequency following the announcement that I was travelling to see the Forbeses.

I refused to feel guilt. I could not say: *It was neither you nor the Queen, or rather it was both, or it mattered altogether too little. I have been alone for a long time.*

I have been alone for a long time.

It is not unreasonable to seek community, to look for comfort. And it is not unrealistic to expect to feel safest with those who have known you the longest. The Forbeses were my family when I was little, when I was most vulnerable, when I knew little else of the world. Nevertheless, I have my own revelations to interrogate. This is not simply a reunion of lost loved ones. I have questions. This notion of being a jewel does not flatter. Nor does the description provide a complete picture. What else took place in the service of my performance as a gift for others? I will not leave that stone unturned. To be deemed a jewel instead of a person is sinister. Is it not akin to the enslaved African who is also deemed the property of others? How different is it really? To be owned is to be owned. An ornament might be prettier than a wagon, but it is just as passive and just as subhuman. My story is filled with flattery, but I am passive still. One is taken here, received there, enjoyed as this or that. And I understand that this is the life of a woman. This is all they can expect in most places around the world. Certainly in the orphanage. Women were made from pliant girls with few hopes, except to gracefully seduce men, preferably those with means, into ... *accommodating* them as wives in a life of endless passivity.

But I am the daughter of active, rebellious monarchs who rejected the yoke of an empire, found a place to feel at home and created a kingdom to protect those who did not wish to be controlled. They could have protected them better with an empire. But they sought not to because they were not in the empire-building business. They sought independence from external forms of control. I am not just a woman, a model of passivity garnished with status, an exiled princess, a royal descendent; I am surely *exempted* from a life of passivity. I am the daughter of rebellious royals, of radical kings and queens. I come from a lineage of defiance. Even my protector is a queen, not a consort. A leader, not a follower.

I have no intention of following anyone or being passive in my own life and, to the extent that I can choose, I will always choose myself and my needs and my questions. So I look to Mary Forbes for answers. I knew as I began my conversation with the Queen that I was not just seeking familiarity. I had questions; I wanted answers. It is not daring or impudent of me to be forthright about my needs. It is not unbecoming of me to even make demands. To descend from a royalty steeped in rebellion is to have defiance in my bloodline.

Heartfelt journals aside, I need to evaluate everything I thought I knew. All that I was told. Not only about how to present myself in this world, how an aristocratic or royal woman might conduct herself, but everything else as well. And it starts with the Forbeses. I have to know everything, so that I can assess things for myself. Which lessons to keep? Which narratives to leave?

The Forbeses will have known who my ancestors were. What did they think of me? How did Forbes speak of me to his wife? What did Mary think then – and now? What words might have been contained in those letters? The anxious questions did not keep my face from pressing against the glass and staring out at the changing scene with jolts of wonder. Was this how I gazed at the Forbeses when I first met them? I have fleeting memories of the acres of land they kept in England that I roamed at will, playing with their children. The train ploughed on, as pale white horses – so far away they could be little blots – dappled the soft grass of unending fields. I wanted to lose myself in this vision. I thought to myself, what might my life look like were I to reside in Scotland? Could I stay in this castle? Could I play with Mary Forbes' young children? But what would follow once playtime was concluded? I am no longer a girl;

73

I have grown up. There will invariably be expectations. Another conversation for me to have with the Queen. I sat waiting, gazing outside, noting that all the planning or the dreaming in the world would not prepare me for Mary Forbes' own response. And I was still uncertain as to what that would look like. And depending on how it took shape, it could determine the length of my trip.

29 April 1861
The Rectory, Palm Cottage
Gillingham, England

When we finally arrived at the station I found myself trembling as I descended from the train carriage. I could not recall if I had been told that she would be collecting me or whether she was to send somebody in her stead. How would I recognize them? How would people respond to me? Why had I not made certain of these things before I left?

I stepped onto the platform, steeling myself. I began to walk, unsteadily, towards what I assumed was the exit. Someone stepped in front of me quickly. I all but jumped. My body stood still, but my shoulders seemed to fly. I blinked, startled. Before me was a slender woman with dark hair the colour of cocoa, shades darker than my skin. Her eyes, flecked with jasmine, were otherwise as green as the hills, and the vivid white spaces around them lit up an otherwise tired and sunken face.

"Oh Bonetta, *Bonetta*." The words were the echo of a memory.

It was her. It was Mary.

How long had I spent dreaming about this moment? I do not know how I answered. I cannot quite piece together what followed. But in her first glance, I caught something. I saw something I immediately recognized. Something I had not seen for many years, something I did not know I had lost. It was a look. A clear and undeniable look. It held that which we render complex, made so simple. It was a look of pure, uncomplicated love.

Elizabeth would later ask me over and over to tell her what our first words to each other were as Mary and I stood on the platform at the station. We looked at each other. Speechless at first. And then we spoke. I could not say who spoke first. Did she really call my name? Did we just gaze and gaze at each other? I must have told Elizabeth something, but I assume I gave her a plausible but fictional account. I cannot recall how I went from the platform to the castle, and then to the chamber where I lay my head every night for over a month. Though we talked at length, the details still elude me.

I, so often perceived as cold by the Schoens, was as emotional as she. We both cried. On the platform but at other moments too. I confess that certain patterns struck me that I did not disclose to Elizabeth. Mary was very affectionate. *I appeared to enjoy this.* I accepted it from her, as I did from few others. Mary was also very tired. I think I had … forgotten, perhaps, the extent to which being a widow would have determined the entirety of her life going forward. On select topics she was reluctant; on others, her words were hesitant. It was clear, for one reason or another, that she did not like the Queen. She would not be persuaded to admit this or to explain why. But she was not interested in hiding her displeasure.

By contrast, when I was disgruntled, when I made an impertinent remark about the Queen, Mary would be quick to chastise me and remind me of whom I was speaking. "You are more of a royal orphan than a royal child," she would say in a dry tone. "Your royal connections come from this queen. Your security, your safety, everything. You must not forget this; you may think as you choose, but outwardly you need to recall the magnitude of what she has done for you and conduct yourself in line with that." It was not the kind of comment I could expect from Elizabeth. It is hard to say why. But it felt different. We would be seated in the Buttery, which Mary alone would use. She would chide me and then take a freshly made hot toddy and place it into my hands. I would accept it and she would hold on for a moment, so that my hands were held by hers. Her hands were firm and strong. She was not tall. Somehow in my head she had been tall and thin. But in person she was not. Nor was she small. She was strong. Lithe. With the body of one who lived an active life. The air in Scotland seemed so clear, one could not imagine it being better in heaven.

I thought back to the grounds for shuttling me off to Sierra Leone after we had lost Forbes. My poor lungs were in urgent need of fresh air, and the climate of Africa as experienced through an orphanage

2,500 kilometres from my first home was thought to be the perfect option! Might they have been mistaken? Might breathing the air here and remaining with the family I then had have been better solutions than ferrying me back and forth across continents, with the promise of loneliness as the only constant? Emotions aside, the Scottish air was wondrous. I do not think I coughed once. It was quiet though. Her children were not around. I wondered about this. She made an allusion to them having felt ignored and sad. Grief of their father compounded because I, too, was taken from them at the same time.

"Would a reunion be good for them?"

She sighed, sitting by one of the fireplaces in the Great Hall one evening. It was rare that we sat in the hall. She preferred the smaller rooms for obvious reasons, given how large the castle was and how few companions she had. The hall felt forlorn. The absence of her family was so heavy it was almost tangible. Windsor Castle never felt like this. Even with people siloed off in their respective wings, it always felt *lived in*. I could not say the same here. But it did feel much more intimate. To be ignoring the function of such a room and instead getting cosy by the fire was subversive somehow. Mary led the way by sitting fully on the floor, legs crossed, wearing what I assume was Forbes' old trousers and a collarless waistcoat. Her hands rubbed the hot toddy in front of her and she looked into the fire, lost in thought. I had not seen her wearing men's clothes before. It was not until much later that I remembered how frequently she did this over the course of my stay. It was a habit of hers, a practice that began at night when the servants had retired to their sleeping quarters. It was the kind of conduct that could cause gossip, and yet, try as I might, I could not read rebellion into it. I read grief. She was wearing her departed husband's clothing. To me she was wrapping herself in his memories. It was the impetus behind it that prevented me from seeking some spare trousers to wear for myself. I envied her departure from the tight bodice I felt so stifled in; I did so in silence.

Her voice was low as she went on. "It may not have even been good for you. I could not predict how they would reply. It seemed unfair that you might shoulder the burdens of their pain in response to the silences you did not cause but they held you accountable for. They had wondered about you; they had hoped to hear replies to my letters. They could not grasp the reason for your silence."

I did not know what to say. I watched her. I listened.

I wondered once more about the motives of the Queen, but it was not something I thought I would ever be able to bring up. Even with Mary, this topic placed us on fragile footing. We were on safer ground when we talked of her former husband: the great navy man, Forbes. She had kept or filled the family rooms with ... well, he was everywhere. The various wings of the castle, set aside for daily use or that of guests, did not resemble what one might expect from a clan or a noble house that has since lost its patriarch, or any woman long widowed, albeit widowed young. The castle looked like a place Forbes was set to return to, honouring him in his absence, while he was out at sea, serving his queen and country. His memory, his presence, was everywhere – in the most unexpected places. In the Great Hall and the secondary one, for every painting of the Forbes clan there were several additional ones of him. Most, it seemed, were taken from a single photograph. There was so much photography. He was captured on film in a few images, and then there appeared to be prints made of the same, which were upon every mantelpiece, but also in bed-chambers in the various guest wings. Photographs and notebooks and trinkets and administrative notes to him or from him littered the boudoirs and women's drawing rooms. She would direct my attention to them before I could even point them out. Indeed, her action dispelled what might have sounded like concern from my tongue. She would then smile the kind of smile that ... one might opt to live a thousand painful nights before enduring the kind of hard-ship that would elicit so tragic a smile. After seeing that smile resurface as Mary traced an absent hand over the framing of a print she kept in the kitchen, my thoughts landed on the Queen and Prince Albert. There were perhaps some who would conclude that a life without the tragedies – or rather the intimacies – that produced smiles quite so pained were not lives worth living.

"We were so very in love," Mary began once, unprompted. One was always made to feel like most marriages were loveless, practical things. Perhaps that is indeed the case. But the women I knew, every single one of them, would describe their marriage as a love match. They seemed that way from the outside too. Well-matched couples who would never have settled for convenience. Marriage was done for love, or it was not worth doing at all.

Mary had herself come from noble stock. "We chose each other," she had said to me. "Yes, it was uncommon among our peers. We had married for love. We knew it would be for life. We knew we would feel the same way right until the end."

I never quite knew how to participate in this conversation. I sensed it was less of an exchange than an opportunity for her to speak forth the affection for him, which I doubt she could subject her children to. I wondered what kind of great love is sustained when one person is on a ferry for up to, and indeed over, a year at a time. How long had Forbes been away before he returned with me, another child for her to add to her brood? How would I have felt about that, were I her? But I could not ask these questions. She was not in the place where she could think through the realities of her history. She may never be.

She did not ask me if I had someone I loved in my life. I was grateful. It is a question I will soon have to think about. Yet I would not know where to begin. There are so many aspects to this situation that would be unknown. And the prospect of having a suitor found for me smells of the passivity I am seeking to avoid. These thoughts would recur throughout the month I spent there. On my third night at Castle Forbes, ideas around marriage found me pacing without pause. I was retiring to the rooms that were made up for me, in a guest wing adjacent to her own. Or so I thought. In practice I was just ascending and descending the same three staircases over and over again, without realizing I was not advancing and was actually lost. My pride chafed at being lost. I have spent almost all my life in and out of castles. There is often a trick to navigating them, certainly those made within a particular era, not unlike palaces designed by a single architect or to emulate a particular design. But this castle was unfamiliar. I had not been to Scotland before and thus I had not been to Balmoral, the Queen's most recent acquisition in this country. There is little point, according to the Queen, given the renovations she has ordered, but I was privy to some sketches made by the architect for the transformations she wishes to take place. I want to claim I see similarities in certain flourishes here, but my memory of the Balmoral redesign is weak.

Mary's home, with its narrow, arched lancet windows, small protruding bartizans and ornate corbelling, was also marked by an uneven roof line, as though the towers were stacked on rather thoughtlessly, in stark contrast to the rest. As such, it was different from what I understood about English castles, even English palaces. But note, when I say castles, I do just mean Windsor – castles I visit with frequency, anyhow. Windsor Castle was the first place I formally visited in England, after settling in at the Forbeses'.

Mary's home, here in Scotland, I suspect because it *is* Scottish and so terribly old, resembles little I have seen. Despite the untidy roofing that looks so jarring against the sky, or the narrow windows surrounded by the tall imperious walls, the sandstone gives it an external warmth to offset the indoor chill. It was welcoming, even if it looked incoherent. It was elegant, but not too fanciful. Much needed repairing, but it was not ramshackle. I had suspected that it was more likely that the whole thing would crumble before Mary thought to repair anything. While it needed repairs, it was not neglected. Quite how she lived there alone without her children, whether they were away at school or simply sent to family as of this month, I could not imagine.

She seemed to have more than enough resources, I presume, left to her by Captain Forbes, but even this was not quite explained. Did it keep her busy, I wondered, or did she simply hire people to manage the land for her? I kept trying to envision myself here.

"Could you imagine me here?" I asked on one of my first nights, when we were in what she declared was her favourite room. It was in another guest wing and appeared to be an untouched library. It became hard to tell. Mary made a strong hot toddy and delivered it unasked for; she would grow to make a habit of this, throughout my stay. I started to suspect it was the only drink she could make. Either that or it was the only way she felt able to consume all the whisky she wanted without attracting concern. There was a small fire and the room was warm. I had come down from my wing with a book I had been reading since I arrived. Confronted with an array of shelves, I wondered with regret how I was to read this to the end, when so many dust-covered options were just within reach. What it must be like, to live with so many books!

My eyes stared round the library at the floor-to-ceiling bookcases. "Could you have seen it?"

Mary looked uncomfortable for a moment. "Bonetta," she said, "it would have been irresponsible of me as an adult, as a parent, to dissuade you from your choices. Yes, it would have made more sense to me for you to stay with us. I certainly felt that you would have been more at home here. And this time, it would have been a grieving experience shared. But I understand entirely why you felt differently at the time."

I stopped. Startled. I did not choose to go to Freetown.

"I thought differently?" I repeated with polite surprise. "Well, what did I say to you?"

She paused. "You did not, and nobody betrayed your confidence." She almost looked defensive, protective even. "I think it was fair that, in a world where you have had so much taken from you, your needs listened to your wants at the time. I did think, as a parent and as your guardian in practice, that I knew better. And it's a statement that many parents get to make to their children. But I was not your parent. You were not even our ward. You were the Queen's, and she lets you be the arbiter of your own fate, which I greatly respect. Even if selfishly," and here her voice did seem to almost break a little, "I would have wanted you with me."

But I did not get a choice in the matter.

I wanted to say it aloud: *I did not get a choice in the matter.*

Nobody told me you wanted me to stay. Nobody told me you wanted me to stay.

Nobody let me feel I had any say, that I could make a decision for myself.

I wanted to say these words. I wanted to shout them out loud. I wanted an audience with the Queen. I wanted all three of us to be present. I could imagine the world where I tell Mary the truth. Where we have a moment of deep realization and in the shock we embrace. We bond. We understand each other better than before. We partner in new defiance. I stay in Scotland.

The story writes itself.

But that is not my story. I did not say those words. I remember I was tired. The words I spoke were few and forgettable.

"I can hardly remember that time. The things that I wanted – what I may have said," I added like a coward. "What does the grieving child know about anything?"

She smiled at me, a different tragic smile.

"I suspect your instincts were correct," I continued. "I would have liked for them to have been adhered to – had I known of them."

"Had you known—" she began to say, but already I was changing the subject.

"I should love to hear more about Forbes from you." My voice rode over hers, painting over that moment with a brighter pivot and to her favourite subject. I knew she would acquiesce. "Perhaps later during my stay, you can tell me more about what he said to you. Regarding when he found me. I have the Queen's recollection. But I trust there is more to the story and an unmatched depth of sincerity to the insights you were privy to."

"We can certainly ... yes." Mary's voice was less chipper than mine, and less chirpy than she tended to be when invited to muse on Forbes for no reason.

"How delightful!" I rose to my feet. "With your permission..." I inclined my head and began to withdraw.

Scotland continued to surprise me. It was warm for one! Well, I shall not overstate things. It is warmer than I would have expected. I was also busy, excited and entertained throughout the stay. I settled into a regular routine of being well fed, consuming unusual dishes that were local delicacies, learning how to ride horses, listening to and accompanying the farmers to whom she leased land, learning about agriculture and stealing some quiet moments in that guest wing's library that overflowed with unopened books.

And so, despite there being just two of us, there was always something to engage with and some excitement to be had. It made sense to me, at last, how she might not be lonely here. During this time, to my relief, we spoke little about the past.

Mary also happened to be a painter. "Not professionally," she would insist, but she did have a studio within the castle that she let me explore. She let me use her oils; I had never painted with oils before. She wanted me to explore the depths I had inside. She had me dress up and take a number of photographs. We did this numerous times throughout, but it felt like a single occasion. Like we were capturing a particular single moment. And while photography was something I had experienced before, it had never been done with this level of intimacy by someone who cared for me, and saw *me*, as a person rather than as a curious fact of history. The warmth of late March felt rather like a strange gift in itself, certainly nothing we got in England, and I was determined to make the most of it as often as I could, even if that meant painting by the window, which was not necessarily encouraged. But I wanted to capture the sunlight. I just wanted to bathe in the sky.

One morning, a couple of weeks after I had arrived at the castle, I woke earlier than usual. The sun hung low like jelly in the sky and I went outside barefoot like a child to enjoy the early, empty, beautiful silence of the natural world. I returned slowly, feet damp with the dew, and wandered into the pantry closest to the walled garden. It overlooked my bedroom window; many a morning had begun with me venturing down to the pantry and eating snacks with kitchen maids. That morning Mary showed up and joined me, taking my elbow and leading me to the morning room.

"I think…" I started. There was something in her gaze that made me falter. "I wanted to ask, did he keep a journal about me? Did he … are there records, notes on his thoughts, about meeting me at that time?"

Mary breathed deeply through her nose. "He kept a diary. He always kept one, but it wasn't frequent. When he met you, however, he was quite diligent. Would you like to see it now?"

After breakfast, we proceeded to a room in the East Wing, which I had not seen thus far. Even in a castle that was filled with his medals, his awards, his favourite books, his clothes, his sporting equipment, some *more* photography, this room, with its meticulous recordkeeping, seemed more *his* than any other room in the castle. This was his bedchamber. This had been where Captain Forbes slept. While I knew they would have separate designated bedchambers, I did not think these would be in different wings of the castle, and I assumed they might have had a solar that they both used. But no. It did not seem prudent to ask. I did wonder to myself about the stories we tell. Was the couple sleeping in different bed chambers in different wings of a fortified castle the picture of eternal love that Mary implied? Or was I projecting? Was true love more nuanced than wanting to see someone's face first thing in the morning each day? Was this not the same husband she was without for months at a time during his life? I was judging, and judging based on a complete absence of information. I knew better.

She showed me the diary. His writing. Familiar yet unfamiliar. I had not seen it in many years.

The words with which he describes me, the detail he goes into ... like I am a puzzle to be figured out: a wonder that was falling from the sky.

As I was flicking through it and she was looking over my shoulder, had I ever felt so simultaneously special and strange? I closed the diary and held on to it. I turned to her. She stepped back with surprise, like she was not expecting me to turn just then. She gasped. We were both a little out of breath. "May I ... may I keep this?" I asked her, my tone wavering. "May I take it to my bedroom to read later?"

"Well, yes, of course," she insisted with anxious relief. I wondered what it was she thought I was going to say.

Perhaps she thought I wanted to keep it for good. But something in her relief told me that there was something else that I had missed, some reason I would find, that would leave me less enthused. It is the kind of information that is almost impossible to ask for. What exactly might I say? I glanced over the diary. I opened it once more, flicked through the pages.

"You are correct about his diligence," I said, my smile weak. She looked at it lovingly.

"He was never this diligent," her voice broke. "He knew."

He knew?

"He knew what?" I asked.

Mary coughed. "He knew that this was one of those experiences. He knew this was not something he would ever want to forget. He knew this to be something most people never live to see. He knew the importance of those early memories. So he wrote every moment; he wrote every moment down."

Importance? Her choice of word might have made more sense had I had the chance to read the diaries. But I had not. Nor could I understand how something so important could have remained inaccessible for almost a decade. I struggled with how to say that kindly. I settled for something more diplomatic.

"What a shame, then, that they were unread." I chose a soothing tone, sprinkled with regret. "I feel as though he did not get to manifest the dream of their importance."

Mary looked at me, her face blank. "Unread?"

"I have not read them."

"Yes, you h—" Mary paused. "You have not. Of course. But you are within the diaries. It was…" She smiled at me for a moment. "Bonetta, remember all your news stories, all those papers that sought to talk to you. They got their insights from his words. This is how you became famous, why you were featured in all these high-society outlets. It was because of his words. They *were* read."

I looked at the diary. "This diary does not look like it has been touched for quite some time." I wasn't sure how I felt. I was trying, struggling, it appeared, to make sense of what was being said.

"Yes, well..." She paused. "When he passed, you were taken too. And even if you had not been, I would have had little desire to recount your narrative. It was done with joy. Initially. To keep writing without you there ... I could not write *his* diary. I could not write *for* him. I was consumed by my grief over having lost him. I could not process my grief about him publicly, so..."

"Publicly?" I began to understand. "So he wrote this diary and made it available for public consumption? He sold his diary. He sold my story?" I could not quite keep the disgust out of my voice.

"No, no, no!" Mary interrupted me. "He did not sell his diary. He took select insights from the diary and made those into a book. The book is a polished version of the real events, but it would not have existed without the diary. The diary is where you see what he truly thought about you. The book is merely the story that he told to the world of your extraordinary life, your extraordinary existence. *Extraordinary*." Her voice was feverish now. I felt the weight of her worldview being pressed upon me. I was to see it her way.

Extraordinary? It was an extraordinary secret. I paused. Was the nobler approach to hold my tongue? Withhold the extent of my displeasure? Opt not to make it clear how unflattering, how exploitative I found this new revelation. Forbes had published a book about my life without my knowledge, without my permission, without me even seeing the contents. Once more I was a product for exchange; my life was to trade.

"What I have heard thus far," I said, in a tone with almost no inflection, "is an account of how my life has now served as fodder for his literary ambitions."

She recoiled. She actually recoiled. She had not done this. But she had felt the sting of my distaste; I had poisoned the well of grief, caused her pain and tarnished her hero, for a grievance that took place over a decade ago and was committed by someone who was now dead.

By her sensibilities, I was not allowed to be angry. To express an entirely reasonable response. Unbidden, the question of the Queen removing me from their household resurfaced in my mind. Had she found the architect of this crude manoeuvre a disappointment and, in his death, removed me from them all? I did not say this to Mary. I handed the diary back. I made my excuses. Left quickly. Promptly got lost and spent much of the day stumbling into progressively emptier and colder rooms, arid spaces haunted by the smell of the forlorn. I imagined myself living here, having my life squeezed like milk from a cow for insights that could be fed to newspapers as exciting new stories. I thought about my birthday and laughed a mirthless snicker into the chilly air. Had they heard I had been forgotten by the Queen when I came of age, would this not have found its way into every society title and printed story they could find? My shame held up for all to consume, like my life. Everybody I had once known would have heard how I was rejected, exploited and unwanted on my birthday while they pocketed the pennies they did not need but keenly extracted as the price of their revelations.

The next two weeks were something of a blur. I was reading a lot in my room. I sought solo activities more than anything else. I would go outside to be with the horses, cleaning them out, which was not unpleasant. It was quiet, necessary, and I grew so fond of those beautiful beasts. It was a practice better conducted alone. And then apropos of nothing, I received a telegram on behalf of the Queen. I had been summoned to St James's Palace. Relief clashed with irritation. Summoned here, I must pack at once and leave; sent there, and off immediately I should go. Meanwhile, all that can be extracted from me is sold to newspapers behind my back – stories about me that I had not read or known were being told. Stories told by whom I did not know. How much of that first fateful trip that I cannot recall was captured in Forbes' diary and peddled to every gentleman in England who could read? I wanted to burn that diary. Or I could have collected it and taken it with me. I chose not to. I wanted nothing from the Forbeses. I was the gift. I could not expect to be the recipient. Nor need I stay. I had the insights I had sought. Now to return to the Queen who had ordered it so, with dread hovering over my heart, wondering if this news would send it spiralling into my stomach. Or maybe I would always live feeling slightly weighted. Navigating life as the world was preternaturally dark.

I had to steel myself to say goodbye to Mary. It was about the second week in April. I had stayed for nearly a month.

"I have my summons!" I told her one morning when I caught her making herself breakfast in the pantry that sat below my bedroom window. I waved the telegram like a shield. I felt guilt, guilt at my relief.

She fixed me with a hard stare. "Families can wrong each other; what matters is how they make amends later."

I nodded, my head bowed.

"I cannot defend a dead man's choices. It is not fair to him or me. You are entitled to your feelings as well, but I have to honour his memory. I cannot feel shame for something he regarded as his pride and joy. He saw himself as your guardian, as a keeper of your extraordinary history. You entering his life was a gift."

"People are not *gifts*. Gifts are forms of property."

"You have never heard children described by their own parents as a gift?"

I did not answer.

"I will have a stable boy take you to the station. Send me your address when you return."

"I shall."

"Bonetta. I want to write to you. I want us to continue ... to remember our deep bond and continue to connect in the future."

I could not answer. I was taken to the train station in silence. I was more informed than when I had left for Scotland, and deep down I wished I knew much less.

3 May 1861
The Rectory, Palm Cottage
Gillingham, England

I have not been summoned like this before. There is something about it, a summoning. It can be a flattering thing. It could highlight one's importance, or speak to the urgency of what is taking place. Is it about timing? Importance? I can state with confidence I was not feeling very important to others. And to myself? I was being framed, shaped even, in a relative or contingent manner. To put it another way, whether or not I mattered was dependent on other people's needs. My whole life was flattened into the value it offered others. I was relative to others, my "importance" forever to be determined by somebody else's needs, their wishes, their feelings. The recurring sentiment that adulthood has brought is the sense that I am an afterthought. My voice, like the sentiment, was little more than an echo. My feelings are immaterial – if they were ever considered at all.

So when the Queen summoned me to the palace, I knew even before she told me why I was there that it would not be good news. At the very least, it would be something I did not want to know, or that which I did not care to do. And given the nature of the summoning, it was not a request or a question. It was an announcement, most likely, followed by an instruction.

She was late. She had summoned me but was not available when I arrived. To make me feel a little special, I jest. A courtier instructed me in cool tones to wait outside the smaller drawing room. I could not wait inside. I have *never* been asked to wait outside. And in the hallway, there was nowhere to sit. I raised this.

I had arrived with only a sliver of patience, and the courtier turned to me with a wolfish smile and said, "Even princesses can stand, Lady Forbes. I am sure you can endure waiting for five minutes on your feet. It is for your protector, Her Majesty, after all."

Five minutes? I stood for an hour.

I had been ordered back from Scotland to stand and stare at the boiserie on a wall. As there were no windows in this hallway, I was in the dark, even during the day, until the Queen finally arrived. I felt like a puppet subject to minor indignities to amuse an idle audience. It is not hyperbole. It felt absurd. How else might one explain this pattern?

When the Queen arrived, she was escorted past me in silence, a silence she maintained until I followed her into the room and we were both seated. She did not mention Scotland nor ask how the trip had been. She inquired neither about Mary nor the castle. Had she any questions about the trip's impact on my person? As to whether the sense of family that I had so ardently sought had been found in Scotland? She neither knew nor cared. One would think she did not know I had travelled. I slumped in my chair, trying to count all the gold accents I saw in the room as a mild distraction.

"You have received a betrothal request, Sally."

There was a long silence. She did not appear to have anything to add. I gazed at her. I stood for an hour for this?

A letter would have sufficed.

The words danced on the tip of my tongue. I pursed my lips. It was not an expression of displeasure. It was an act of self-control. I did not trust myself to speak with grace. Waiting appeared the better course of action than responding. My inner monologue did not foretell great patience.

She placed an envelope face down on the table between us. It was cream and square with a daub of fat red wax at the centre. The seal was broken, the wax puckered like a kiss. I did not reach for it and so, sighing, she spoke again. "There is a man by the name of James Pinson Labulo Davies who writes of your encounter at the Freetown orphanage. He was charmed by you then and remains so. He lost his first wife and came across a story about you recently in a newspaper. He wishes to be wed and he was reminded of you. He has asked for your hand."

She did not appear to have anything to add.

I did not know this man. I was not curious about him and I did not recognize the name. There was more to the story, I could tell.

If a man just wished to marry me, would the Queen get so involved? Unless she already approved of the man. Or an arrangement had already been put in place. I needed more information. *Or* to see if I could get away with knowing very little.

I tried to keep my voice light. "Was a summons required?"

"Sally?!" *Quelle horreur!*

Oh-ho, a sign of life.

Pride is irrepressible. Few experiences can quell it indefinitely. It would not do to look too excited.

I sat up straighter. "I am not being impetuous. *Au contraire.* I am trying to be considerate. Attending this meeting has clearly caused you some inconvenience, which might be necessary were you in need of my input. Neither my perspective nor my permission has been sought on the matter, however. One might argue that said input appears irrelevant. If it is less an exchange of ideas than a conferral of knowledge, then a letter is a better medium for this, for the service of delivering information. It would not require any additional travel. We were both, it appears, otherwise indisposed."

"Sally, do not overreact."

"Your Majesty," I said slowly. She hates when I call her this. "As ever, I take my cues from my Queen. My voice is an octave lower than yours, and I am speaking in dulcet tones. Where my manner is out of proportion with the topic, I shall gladly be corrected. Or is it my deportment? I was slouched but I have since straightened up."

She frowned. "Sally, you are frightfully smart. Wonderfully bright. It is your great gift. But you wield it in a manner most unbecoming of your station. And most disrespectful of mine."

I did not care. But one of us would have to capitulate and it would not be her.

She continued, her tone growing ever more clipped. "Your parlour games shall not be tolerated here. We speak with candour or not at all. You are angry because, as you have claimed, your perspective has not been sought."

The air between us was truculent. I did not agree; I did not disagree. I knew better than to admit any truths to the accusation that I, apropos of nothing, was angry.

We sat in silence and then she leaned forward and said in her softest voice, "Why are you here, do you think?"

"This is the first real question you have asked me!" I said in a flash. *It was rhetorical.* But somehow I could not help myself. I was raw. I was not in control. It was present in her eyes as she gazed back at me.

The anger I had felt for months was leaping forth unbidden. I continued, "To which I shall answer with the candour you insist upon. I do not know what you seek from me at this point. I do not know why I am here. Candour from all would suit the situation, I suspect."

Her eyes narrowed. "He is currently in England and I have invited him for tea."

Information that could have been sent in a letter. A voice sang in my head: *My opinion has not been sought.*

In the ensuing silence, she all but snapped, "Can I count on your presence, Sally?"

"Is it compulsory?"

The Queen gritted her teeth. "Yes."

"Well, then, this is hardly a question."

She reddened. I wondered briefly if she had smacked her children before and if that was coming next. I have seen this happen at the Schoens' and even at the Forbeses'. I assumed it would be a governess that would mete out such violence, but the Queen's face seemed fit to burst. She looked keen to throw or hit something.

Perhaps I sought to protect myself.

Whatever the impulse, I burst out, "I am hardly being impertinent. This *would* be best placed in a letter. You are giving me instructions. We are not conversing!"

"Sally, why are you so ill-mannered today?" The Queen rose to her feet. For a moment, I thought she would ring her bell and have me escorted out. The alarm must have flashed across my face because something mellowed in hers. "Sally, this was planned with ... care."

She began to pace the drawing room. I did not know if I should join her. I sat, watching as she walked back and forth, words sailing over her shoulder.

"This is a man who speaks your language. He comes from your

continent, from your tribespeople. He is wealthy and wishes to make you his bride. When did you last even speak to somebody who came from your own region? With all your talk about feeling alone, foreign, removed, other, I really thought this could not have come at a better time."

Yes. Fine. But still. "Why was I not consulted from the start?"

"Sally."

"You know how unsettled I am by surprises."

"Sally, you do not need to be forewarned about a conversation. You are an English lady, an African princess. You can interact with other human beings and present yourself socially. You were trained to do this. Furthermore, this pouting of yours is unbecoming. *It shall cease at once.* Tea at this palace with Mr Davies shall take place three weeks from now and we shall have two dresses made, from which you will choose one. We are not granting any more time to this. You are meeting a possible suitor. You will engage him in conversation. You are of age; this is what happens."

"And should I dislike him, following the tea?" I paused, realizing something. "Tea at the palace is not something you offer every suitor, I imagine. How much choice do I have in this matter?"

The Queen fixed me with a gaze. Her patience looked thinner than mine. She said, "A single meeting over tea is not sufficient to make lasting judgements. And tea at my palace does not require anyone *else's* consent. Tea with you, my ward and protégée, tea with a young lady one wishes to wed and her guardian is not so extraordinary that it requires consent or approval. If any is required, then I have granted it. You are correct that tea here at St James's Palace is a strong sign. I have had this man looked into. We had to make sure he would be worthy of your time. He has proved a respectable, impressive man from our investigations. He has a fortune befitting the spouse of a princess and, while he lacks a lineage, he was born to free parents, has significant assets and, most of all, shares your heritage."

Said like that, it rather felt like I was being betrothed to my own brother. I suppressed my shudder. A surviving member of my family would be more welcome, especially a man to restore the monarchical line. What did I even know of such things? Simply that her emphasis on 'heritage' was rather too close for comfort. But the alternative was hardly inspiring. Mr Davies wedded to Princess Aina? The commoner rises in his station, but what becomes of mine? Would I be better off should Mr Davies prove to be a sibling of mine? Not quite the family reunion I sought, one where I donned a wedding gown to marry myself in male form. Maybe a mere relative? Like dear Prince Albert? My mind wandered away to these merry, absurd, but altogether more exciting flights of fancy. But she was still speaking...

"And most of all, he is simply asking for an opportunity to meet. I see no harm in the matter."

Well, of course she saw no harm. He was not to marry her or her daughter. And of course, he had read a story about me – I am written about; I am engaged with; I am so *passive* in my life. If I do not like him, what happens then? I did not say this. I had asked already. She had made it clear. I would keep meeting him, until like him I did.

8 May 1861
The Rectory, Palm Cottage
Gillingham, England

I did meet him, James Pinson Labulo Davies, the African naval philanthropist. And, well, where to begin? We met in the tea garden. Here, it was a warm day. I was not excited. I was, I felt, on display. There have been many moments where I have actively been on display!

The Queen would bring me to the palace or Windsor Castle and allow me to sit in on an event or an interaction with a diplomat or with a foreign man who in other spheres would be called unkind names. She would have me sitting there, the picture of opulence, wearing borrowed jewels and speaking in my accent, which appears to dazzle so many people, Britons and foreigners alike. And naturally, they are curious and intrigued. And there was something about my manner that makes it clear I'm not a prop, which is to say: this is not for show. Well, it is for show, but it is not pretend. I do come here often, I speak to the Queen often, I am comfortable in regal clothing, *but it is so very uncommon to be presented for that purpose.*

I resent being deemed a mere spectacle, even as I enjoyed meeting the interesting men that the Queen entertained. But my meeting with James was supposed to be for my benefit. He was my suitor, or being brought so I might consider him as such. It seemed prudent that he should be on display rather than me. This was not the case, however.

Thus, on the day early in May when I was sent to the palace to meet James, a carriage was sent for me, a *two-horse* brougham. Arriving at the palace, the guards were cheerful. Whether they had been told to be or they had heard the gossip, who can actually say. Either way, I was ushered through and my beauty, my outfit, was remarked upon.

I was hurried into a more discreet sitting room; the Queen was already there with this James. I did not recognize him despite our apparent meeting in Sierra Leone so many years ago. He sat with his back perfectly straight, his dark, gleaming eyes half turned to his china cup, half focused on the Queen. I was a little surprised. I thought *he* was the guest du jour; would it not have been better for him to encounter the Queen and me at the same time? Instead, I felt rather like I was on the wrong side of a formal dinner. The courtiers may well have been waiters at my back, offering me up as a dish to be considered. Well, there I was – and there he was. His gaze was impenetrable as it landed on my person.

And the Queen, who had been doing a remarkable job of seeming engaging and engaged, looked at me, and her face seemed to fall. She was crestfallen. I could not tell why. Was it the outfit? Was it my expression? Perhaps all those eager comments about how I looked like such a *swan*, a *rose* – pick a compliment – were hollow words typical of one's social inferiors. And when presented with someone who is not, you see the honesty about who you really are and how you really look. After all, they have nothing to lose. And she looked at me like she had lost everything, just by staring into my face.

James was suitably deferential to the Queen. He laughed whether her jokes were funny or not. And he did so in a manner that did not seem obsequious. The laughter was discreet. A certain chuckle behind the hand, a slight touch of discretion here and there. Perhaps something wasn't funny, but he was indulging her. Perhaps it was funny, but it was not a good practice to laugh so loudly. Either way, he played his part perfectly. And somehow it made me sick. I had never really encountered a man like him or a situation like this. Usually an African man who was meeting with the Crown had some agenda specific to their own country. It was rare that they were meeting to essentially build a personal alliance, and in this situation it was in order to get to me...

Well, I just did not know what to think. Were they to get along, would that matter? In truth, I had never been privy to the conversations the Queen had had with the various families she had pulled together to take care of her young ward, whether it was the Forbeses or the Schoens or the handmaidens in between. This kind of conversation, where you speak to the chaperone or the would-be suitor or the caretaker of the orphan girl, was something I was unfamiliar with. And here, I was witnessing a snippet of it in real time. After some forgettable conversation over china in the tearoom, in which I mostly sat silently, he and I took a chaperoned walk. The chaperone was somebody I did not even know, which belies the point really of there being one. The Schoens had wanted to come. They were discouraged, I was later told.

And as we walked around the gardens, I saw a different version of the man who had charmed the Queen.

He asked me questions in a manner that presumed unflattering answers. "Do you speak your native tongue? It is Yoruba, is it not?"

"It is," I said, unaware as to whether it really was or not. Nobody had told me. And I obviously could not remember. It did not seem like a useful thing to state. So instead I faltered, but my tone grew a little remote.

"Well, of course, I could not possibly still speak the language, could I?"

He looked at me with a face devoid of obvious expression. I could smell the judgement, nevertheless.

"Everyone in my family is dead."

He opened his mouth and closed it again. He looked embarrassed.

I continued. "Do you think that the Englishman is going to have a working knowledge of Yoruba? That they might educate me in the language?"

"Well," he said, stumbling over his words, "I was told that your ... your caretakers, the Reverend and his wife, were multilingual. I suppose, from the perspective of an Englishman, multilingual does not include African tongues."

"They speak many African tongues!" I snapped.

"But you do not speak any."

"I have no interest in speaking African tongues that are not my own."

"But you have not made an overwhelming effort to master the one that *is* your—?"

"Have you lost anyone?" I demanded, my tone icy, and something clicked in his eyes that told me that perhaps he had. I realized belatedly that, yes, of course, he had been a soldier or naval officer. He had taken some sort of job that sent men overseas, promised violence and involved people dying. And of course, he had been married before. His first wife was dead. So, yes, he had. But before he could dismantle my hubris with the extent of his own personal losses, before he could say anything at all, reveal either a pouting arrogance, or a masterful grace, I continued with careful specificity.

"Do you, James, know what it is to lose your entire family before you can hold on to the memories of their names?" I did not think so.

We had been walking. He stopped. He stared at me and shook his head.

Good. I was a little surprised. He had met me at an orphanage in the first instance. Did he think I had lived until that very moment with my family? Had he not read news stories about me?

I straightened my shoulders and continued to walk. My face looked ahead. There were many conversations I would be happy to have. The conversation in which I am interrogated about the extent to which I have capitulated to an English way of life, and thus neglected the roots of my heritage, is not one I will tolerate with somebody who cannot conceive of the life that I have lived. Certainly not from somebody whose 'exciting life' is entirely of their own making, whose life has been shaped and driven by their autonomy from beginning to end.

He was hurrying to catch up with me, and out of the corner of my eye I could see his head was somewhat bowed. "You cannot know what my life has been like. At best, you can imagine that one would not choose willingly to be parted from all they knew and held dear, from the continent where they would be seen as a human being, to be gaud, gift, garnish ... but never a real girl. A foreigner in an English country. My life has been wholly without choice and far beyond your comprehension. This is something you should do well ne'er to forget."

We were walking side by side once more and he nodded in mute acquiescence. He looked humbled. He also looked unimpressed.

I was unconcerned with this. I was not doing it to impress him. I was holding in my temper. I continued to glance at discreet moments in his direction. It was not quite resentment or indulgence that remained as we walked on in silence. But the feeling that emanated from him could be seen to sit on that spectrum. He was making allowances for the emotional outburst of a child. It was the performance of patience. It was pride. Any possible conversation had withered at this point.

I did not wish to talk to him. "I am cold."

"Yes," he agreed with vigour. "Yes. Perhaps we should return inside."

"That would be best."

We did not speak again.

The Schoens were thrilled when I returned. Before I could open my mouth to speak, Elizabeth all but jumped on me.

I often used to wonder if my dolls were waiting for my presence to lift them from stillness to life. When I entered the kitchen, the Schoens looked rather similar: there they were, lifeless, motionless, like dolls when a child has stopped playing with them. Spotting me, they awakened.

"What was he like?"

"Is he handsome?"

"Is he wealthy?"

I looked over the heads of the children to Elizabeth. Surely she ought to curtail this. Her eyes were as wide with curiosity as the rest of them. "Sarah is tired," she said. "Let her rest."

I could not help but gaze at her in surprise; she was not calling me Sally today, not forcing affection, oblivious to my discomfort. Does she understand me better than I used to think? Or is my sense of exhaustion more than a weary thought in my mind? Elizabeth put her hand on my elbow because touch is something she cannot resist even at her most thoughtful. I was not repulsed by it today. I let her hand stay there, guiding me with a firmness as she steered us past the family.

"Sarah needs to rest," she repeated.

I could not be certain, but she seemed to have a smile at the corners of her mouth. It was not for me; it was directed at the others. Or so it seemed. I confess I was feeling somewhat weak.

"Let us give her space," she continued, and I felt immense gratitude at her words. I did not utter a sound, even when she came with me to my bedroom and helped put me to bed, pretending almost that she was a lady's maid. I indulged her. I may have even indulged myself.

But no good deed goes unpunished. Once she had me alone, she began to ask her questions. And I found I could not hide my thoughts; I could not lie to her. I was too tired. She was too adept at playing what I sought – mother or handmaid. I was never quite clear on how those roles truly differed. I did not want to talk. But I wanted to be heard or understood by somebody.

"So how did it feel?" she asked. I put on my nightdress, facing away from her. She plumped up the pillows as she spoke. It gave her a reason to remain in the room. It allowed her to keep asking me questions. I didn't answer at first. Then, I heard her sigh and take a breath and realized she may actually repeat the question, which would be embarrassing for us both. I would start to lose my patience with her.

I tried to steel myself and speak with calmness, but the moment I began, the rage rolled out. "How did it feel?" I repeated. "Well first – *first...*" and she stopped and looked up with expectation. "He ... he looked down on me. And he made that clear. He looked down on me!"

Something in my indignation must have told Elizabeth not to bother suggesting an alternative perspective. She said simply, "Well, that is easy enough to convey to the Queen; is it reason enough to turn someone down? I would say it should be."

"But I do not know that I have a slew of other suitors waiting," I confessed. The words slipped out.

"What does the Queen think about this?" Elizabeth, stunningly uninformed, somehow knew not to dwell on the revelation lest I withdraw. She carried on in a brisk tone as though I had not exposed myself in a moment of weakness, of shame, of desperation.

"The Queen?" I shook my head. I was staring up at the ceiling of my four-poster bed. "The Queen just told me to speak to Alice. She told me that I ... that Alice would help me see things properly or clearly.

She effectively told me to go away and tell someone who could convince me *out* of my perspective, as opposed to hearing how I felt." I paused.

The words that followed I dared not say aloud. I dared not look down, lest my gaze join the tears that dripped down my chin and onto my lap. All it would take was a blink and I would be looking directly at Elizabeth.

The words floated unspoken above my head: the Queen has sat with me many times discussing Prince Albert. How initially, they seemed to clash. He seemed rude; she was unhappy. And then they fell in love. How hers was a love match. He may have been chosen for her, but they actually fell in love.

How can she not recall how important this was for her and offer me that same empathy? How could she not understand that I would want to choose? Maybe there were not an abundance of suitors, I do not know. But could she, if nothing else, not present this as another certainty? Another destination where this parcel that I have become will just be packed up and sent off. She should know that I want to feel special. I want to feel anchored, to have my feet on the proverbial ground, not to be uprooted and just sent to whomever—

Elizabeth coughed. I heard the intake of breadth that precedes a question. My eyes dried as if on command. I looked at her, but she did not speak.

I would want to feel special. This James character seemed

predisposed to communicate to me that I was inadequate. That what might be special, what might be a curio, what might be *excitement* in this part of the world, was inadequate by the standards of an African man. Do I know my language? Do I speak it? Do I not then speak other African languages? How have I not properly clued myself into all that is African, given that the Reverend speaks African tongues, given that he's lived on the continent, given that I too have lived on the continent.

All these presumptions. As if I have the freedom that he does, as if I have been groomed to expect that I can be heard, that I can be the architect of my own life, when even the opportunity to choose the outfit I wish to wear was something withheld from me for that particular meeting. I had to be dressed in an outfit selected by the Queen.

There was a time when she understood how I felt and, as such, what it felt like to have one's autonomy denied, but not anymore. I did not say this out loud. My words were tamer than that which I let loose in my head.

"Ah, Mrs Schoen," I said. "Alice is getting married. I think she suspects that the perspective will be enlightening for me. And who am I to challenge what ... what I do not already know?"

I could hear Elizabeth clearing her throat wanting to offer some words. But I could not bear the idea. I lay down on the bed, turned on my side and closed my eyes.

"Thank you so much, Mother," I said, knowing the word would

make her feel special. "Thank you for putting me to sleep so kindly."

She put her hand on my shoulder, which was exposed above the duvet. "Goodnight, dear Sally," she said, her hand trembling. She rose from the bed and walked away. She was always so slippery, some-how – too close, too intimate. Like a fly hovering around my ear that never flew very far, no matter how often I swatted it.

Princess Alice was not what I expected. I had spoken to her before, of course. But when I was directed back to the palace to speak with her specifically, I was not sure what the expectations were, what the procedure was. There were the official rules, but as Queen Victoria herself deviated from them in favour of her own personal preferences, was I to expect Alice to do the same? If so, then how was I to interact with her? Could I be seated as I awaited her? Did she require people to curtsy in private with her? Would she expect me to call her 'Your Royal Highness'? Nobody provided any such answers.

The Queen had decided, unilaterally of course, that I needed to spend time with Princess Alice.

You were both born in 1843; you are both of marriageable age. Alice did not wish to be betrothed but, now that she is, she has found her life enriched by it. Prince Albert needs more of my support and it may be

that I cannot see you quite as often. As such, I have arranged for you to
meet with Alice, for some guidance and friendship.

Reading the letter repeatedly did not make the message within it any less awkward. I could not imagine how this would unfold, but at the very least, Princess Alice would have to try and make it less embarrassing than it otherwise would be. Or so I assumed. The Queen actually left the arrangements to her courtiers, which meant I was summoned to Princess Alice's presence. Friendship rarely begins when one person is presented like the royal subject of the other. I was collected from the Rectory, not unlike a parcel, and deposited in whichever palace Princess Alice happened to be in that day. If the footman knew beforehand they neglected to tell me. Instead I would be led from one royal wing of one royal residence through another, directed by one courtier who disappeared and was replaced by another, and eventually I would be told to wait outside a drawing room or a smaller boudoir while either she was fetched or, quite often, simply woke up.

Our first encounter had her meeting me outside a drawing room, where she gave me barely a glance while nodding until the courtier was well out of sight – at which point, she took me by the hand and we skipped through numerous hallways and up the various staircases until we entered a wing where her bed chamber was.

"Well, hello," she said with an impenetrable smile, pushing the door shut with a firm click. "The *mystical* Sally."

"*Mystical*?" I said, with an eyebrow arched.

"To *Mama* you are the genius of geniuses. The ideal firstborn."

"Genius? I am just her favourite brooch."

Alice looked at me wordlessly for a moment, then she trilled. "Sacrilege!"

"Certainly. Someone should hang for it."

"Are you volunteering?"

"Not until I say something really profane."

She doubled over this time.

"Hanging is serious business. You can only do it once. I want to get all the worst things out. *First*."

"Or during?"

"As I swing?" I asked.

Alice chuckled, "There would be little time for speaking."

"Would a rasp even have the right effect?"

Alice shook her head. She was quick to laugh, quick to smile, definitely more cheerful than any person I had met for some time. "You are funny, but we are here for a reason."

"Not to plot our trip to the gallows?"

"Well, yes. Some just call it 'marriage'."

This time I laughed. "You are..."

"Apparently to be your mentor. Mama has found a way to marry you off as well, yes? Are you not excited about it? I suppose you must not be. Mama guards her toys with jealousy. She would not be punting you to me unless she felt that she could not reach you as she used to."

"Well, to be honest," I replied, "I feel more that I cannot reach her."

She looked at me, eyes inquiring. But something told me that I should not tell the daughter about how I could not connect to her mother quite as well as I used to when I am about the daughter's age. Kind as Alice may be, I would feel jealous were I in her shoes. And I was seeking a friend, not a rival.

"I do not like him, I have to be honest. He is just a bit proud."

And she looked at me and laughed again. "Is this the 'philanthropist'?"

"Yes."

"Oh, how nice! He is rich and he is civilized. That must surely count for something."

"Really? Is that what one is seeking? A man who is rich and civilized?"

"I do not know! With the empire, there are not that many rich people. It does not seem like it is a commonplace set of character traits."

"Well," I drawled, "then you must have a *buffet* of options here, given the wealth and, *ahem*, civilization."

It was the kind of comment that would make anyone else feel embarrassed. But Alice simply shrugged it off. Hers was a faith that tended towards joy. There was nothing a smile could not remedy. She seemed to think back over what I had said. And began to chuckle to herself.

"I daresay, there are none too many civilized men here, either. I suspect it is just men. I think civilization is something they are not able to do. The English gentleman is a bit of a myth, you know. I mean, I do not know if you have met my brother Bertie. But he is as far from a gentleman as one can get. They simply do not exist. It is, in fact, a fiction!"

"A fiction we are meant to believe in..."

"Well, all fictions one is meant to believe in – how else can you get through them if you do not buy into the story?"

"Well, when the story is to last an entire life, that becomes quite the ask, don't you think?"

"But would it last the entirety of your life? The one thing I have noticed is that men tend to die before women."

And it was my turn to laugh. "Alice!"

I do not know what I had expected, but certainly not this level of tender cheekiness. That assumed, there was nothing that could not be said, provided it was said in just the right tone with just the right amount of levity. One could sort of get away with it in the end. And there was no presumption of superiority, nor did this turn to competitiveness or even any real snobbery, certainly nothing that could not be jostled out of one with some reflection. It was the first time I spent a long time, a full afternoon, talking with Alice. It was the first of many.

Soon after, I was hurrying to the palace every weekend. How could I explain such a change of heart? In truth Alice epitomized the one thing I lacked most of all: a friend, an actual friend. I would spend the entire weekend staying there with her. Alice appeared to offer me something the Queen never could. I had been deeply lonely for so long and always somewhat out of place. The Queen, now unwilling to entertain me herself but keen to see that I was being entertained, had provided a better answer than perhaps she herself had intended. Alice and I became inseparable and I, for once, could describe myself as truly happy.

The Schoens were not. In fact, they were more than a little unhappy when I mentioned the possibility of being taught by Alice's governess. Alice had floated the idea of her taking over my education. I was excited, but it appeared I was the only one. The Reverend said, "Well then, we shan't see you at all, shall we? Is that the plan? That you shall be there during the weeks as well? Are you just going to move into St James's?" I confess I felt a thrill of excitement at the prospect. Not that I could admit that, not when his tone was so accusatory.

It took me a moment to find an appropriate response. "Are you opposed to me having a friend?"

"Not at all," Elizabeth almost cooed as she spoke over the

Reverend with warm decisiveness. "Not at all." We were standing in their favourite household spot, gathered around the table in the Rectory's kitchen.

"Could you not bring Alice here?"

"Bring Alice here?" The very idea! Alice was not a snob, but it was just absurd.

"Well, you do not have to. Why not take Annie with you, then?"

I frowned. I could not put my finger on it but I felt a sense of misgiving. Annie and I barely speak. We have not spoken for months. We have barely exchanged words. We might pass each other in the staircase. We give each other a wide berth. In what world would I invite her to spend time with my friend and me?

Prior to this, Elizabeth would not have dared to ask that I take Annie with me to a royal palace. But now, of course, the situation has changed. It is no longer the case that I see the Queen for a specific set of formal reasons and the Schoens show themselves as my dutiful but nigh-invisible stewards and guardians. Now that an informal arrangement has organically arisen with my friend the princess, they spy an opportunity. Annie could be propelled into the upper class. I was being manoeuvred by these good Christian village types. They may have travelled the world to condescend to Africans in the name of the faith, but they themselves were naive and transparent in their scheming and unaware that this was so. I would expect better strategy from Annie herself.

I didn't answer Elizabeth. The silence stretched. She looked at the Reverend and he said, "Well, Annie has apologized, has she not? For your squabble, last year."

"For her *language*," I said.

His eyes went hard. "Well, *yes*. That would be the reason for the apology."

I did not sneer. I insist that I did not. It is a word that was levied at me later, but I did not. I certainly turned away, though, and there was no mistaking the dismissiveness in my body language.

And as I started to walk towards the door, I raised my gaze and saw Annie standing silently, watching.

2 June 1861
The Rectory, Palm Cottage
Gillingham, England

I can only assume it is because quite so many things have happened that I am now writing here so often. It is like I am talking to a friend. Last year, by comparison, life appeared to chug along like a steam train as it starts up. This summer, however, has been flooded with a constant stream of events, and yet, perhaps courtesy of the discipline instilled in us at Freetown, I cannot simply skip over large swathes of my time. I have to explain everything, if only for my own peace of mind.

I was spared an occasion to speak to Annie again for a little while, for which I was thankful. However, this little stretch of peacetime was not to last. At the start of May, I received a letter, or rather, Elizabeth Schoen had intercepted my post and given it to me. Prior to my trip to Scotland, when my relationship with the Queen was in the first flush of uncommon strain, she had been on the lookout, with a lack of discretion that felt impudent, for any letters that might come from the royal household.

There are many plausible arguments for why this was the case.

There is certainly enough room within the loose framework of being her ward – or, as she preferred it, her daughter – for her to make claims about how concerns for my future manifested in this maternal protectiveness. I experienced it differently. Her curiosity was more of a preparative inquiry. She needed to determine whether the Queen had really forgotten me and how soon I would get a message or summons.

I knew, of course, that she needed to know what the Queen's neglect meant for her family and their finances. But I let her pretend that her new habit of taking all my letters to 'hold' before I saw them was from love. Enough time had since passed for it to be unnecessary for her to take every letter that was mine and announce to me its arrival – and hover over me as I opened it in her presence. Yet she continued. She would swoop in and collect my post, hold it to her breast, hurry to wherever I was and make a grand occasion out of the whole thing. Her unwelcome proximity had stirred in me a new need for privacy and a new, but suppressed, loathing of her presence.

In any case, the letter in question was not from the Queen and I could tell at once. Contrary to what people may think, the Queen actually writes her own correspondence; she even writes the addresses on the envelopes.

This scraggly writing was definitely not Her Majesty, Queen Victoria's. I said as much.

Elizabeth looked at me, expectant.

It looked like Princess Alice's hand.

I did not say that, but my face clearly said *something*, and when Elizabeth saw this, that I knew who it was, her own expression changed. I wish I had known of its impending arrival and thus hovered nearby to collect it ahead of her when the post arrived for the day. I still do not know what time it arrived. And I confess that fault was all mine. I rather thought such things were beneath me. I wanted to play at being a lady before my life resembled that of one. But here was the penalty: it gave too much power to others.

In any case, Elizabeth found the letter or received it anxiously. Her sticky fingers, sticky from her children doing whatever it is they do, making every room in the house constantly dirty, left their memory on the envelope. In hindsight I wish she had handled it with a glove. But she could not even give me my letter in my own room; rather, she presented it to the dinner table. Yes, *to* it. We eat in the kitchen, in that middle-class way, and there are just so many of us, that we rarely eat all crammed in at once, except when Elizabeth demands it. This tends to happen at least a couple of times a week but especially on Sundays. It hovers between seeming arbitrary and being a ritual. Perhaps it is to serve as a commiseration after the Reverend has bored everyone with his service *or* perhaps to avoid having to endure him for too long on her own. And so, unto the kitchen she came. The evening meal was already served, faces were being stuffed, the room echoing with the sounds of chomping teeth. The boys picked up fistfuls of food or the plates themselves, their mouths galloping like the hooves of errant horses, this world so far from the sphere of the palace. A lady must always have a delicate palate and the dishes she is served must reflect that, the Queen would insist.

Thus I eat little, as always, and am happy to do so. I did not glance at Elizabeth. I was sated by a light supper and sat pressed against other bodies around the table, my presence as light as I could manage, my hand lingering on my favourite teacup. Somehow my mind was at peace; I say this without hyperbole. I really do think I felt a sort of calm since Alice had come on the scene, and more credit to the Queen for it. She had attempted to encourage this friendship many moons before, but I had felt then I needed a mother figure more than I needed a friend. After a certain point one can very well mother themselves; someone should tell Elizabeth Schoen. Not a mother, but a friend, a girl, a princess, a peer was something I had been badly in need of. And what a pleasant change in my constitution Alice's arrival had brought!

Elizabeth placed the envelope on the table between us. Almost immediately, somebody's hand knocked a glass almost onto it. I snatched it out of the way. I knew it was mine; nobody else was getting letters. There was usually so much commotion that nobody would get to speak at length at the table. But this time Elizabeth paused, and her stillness became a performance. I did not respond with words and our shared silence held everybody rapt.

"Well, open it," she said, as if forgetting herself. She added, "I think it is from the Queen."

Looking back, I think she must have known it was not. Her comment was quite bizarre. I had been spending so much time with Princess Alice that it is more likely that she was the one who contacted me. *We* are the friends. This is how girls get along.

Before I opened the letter, I told her: it is not from the Queen.

"Would Alice be writing to you?"

"*Princess* Alice," I said, and the Reverend looked at me. "Let us not get too comfortable," I added. I was not trying to be rude. I was not putting her in her place. It is just a worrying tendency. What has been said once without qualms can be said again with comfort. I just opened the letter, looked up and said, "You are correct. It was from her. She had some words."

"She had some words?"

She did indeed. It was an invitation and a beautiful one. "I do not think I've seen an invitation quite so gorgeous," I confess. "And I've actually been to a number of events held by the palace."

"Is that the wedding invitation?" Mrs Schoen asked, and I remember seeing Annie look up for a moment – the raised jut of her imperious little chin caught my attention.

"It is not," I said.

I would be excited, were it an invitation to the wedding. Princess Alice, however, was not excited about getting married, nor was I keen for her to leave. I was excited for the dresses, for the gowns. But I could not think of losing Alice.

"When are you going to tell us what's in the letter?" Annie asked. "Or what the invitation is for?"

I looked at her with my polite puzzled expression. It is a winning one, far better than anger. And then I spoke.

"I daresay, dear Annie, I can disclose to you the contents of my private correspondence. But I do suspect that I am under no obligation to do so." I spoke words to that effect. Formal, proper. My summary may not be perfect, but it is close enough. "One might even think it a touch untoward that you would ask me to."

She blushed. I was satisfied.

I looked over the letter properly. I confess that I barely had when I first opened it because so many eyes were on me. I had allowed myself to be distracted. But now I saw it was a peculiar little thing. Not a wedding invitation or a royal event or even a direct invitation. It *wasn't* an invitation from Princess Alice, per se, but actually from a young man named Edward. I was not unfamiliar with this particular Edward. His father held one of the few non-royal dukedoms in England. And we had been introduced once before. I was surprised that I was getting a *second-hand* invitation to a dinner party. But it was clarified in the invitation; they did not know my address. And it was Princess Alice's suggestion. She thought we should all gather together on 15 May. I confess I was keen to do so and to more closely acquaint myself with the members of that social circle.

I did not catch Annie's next comment or, if I did, I cannot recall it. No doubt it was suitably sneering, suitably boring, unworthy of merit, something about ... airs, uppityness. As for the details, well, it is tiresome to repeat them. My response to her was no kinder, though I delivered it with more grace. Still, everybody looked stricken. I am not even sure what I said, something about her lack of manners, something about hubris that is innate, not bred. I might have said I pitied her parents for being such well-mannered people who brought forth some kind of goat. I think I went a little ... I will not say over the top, but I was a touch florid. She got under my skin. I rose with my invitation. Retired to bed. Somebody knocked on my door, hours later. I ignored them, closed my eyes. There was something about the freedom to not engage, to not have to have a curt remark, a terse reply. Just the freedom to forget. I promised myself I would hold on to that memory as I rolled over and slept.

It was one of my favourite days in May. The month had just begun, there was cherry blossom on the streets and, in truth, Kent looked quite as beautiful as anything in late spring. But even so, I always sought to be away and my closeness with Princess Alice meant it was easier to make it so. But last month, I was not just running around with Alice; I was meeting her dressmakers. They had made gowns for me before: whenever the Queen commissioned something, it was crafted by the dressmakers she used for her own daughters. But I was rarely present. I might have discussed previously with the Queen what I wanted or looked at fabrics and talked about styles, but the dressmakers never heard from me directly, nor I them. This time, however, we met in person. I had struggled to contain my excitement at how new this all was for me. To my surprise, Alice seemed equally unacquainted with this. I remember wanting to ask her more, but then, of course, we were interrupted by a knock on the door.

"You have a letter, Miss Forbes Bonetta." And I was curtsied to, or maybe it was just to Princess Alice. Either way, Alice and I exchanged looks. "Why is Mama sending you letters when she knows that you are with me? Why does she not just summon us?"

"It is a summons." The courtier spoke from behind us.

Alice dismissed them quickly. We wanted to talk without being overheard.

"Oh, excellent." Alice's voice was heavy with sarcasm. "I expect an instruction. I would not open it if I were you."

"How can I not open it?" I asked her. "That is truly the most fool-hardy thing you have said."

Alice looked at me and burst into tears of laughter. We fell about giggling for a while, envisioning all the consequences for how the Queen would respond to my silence – so small and slight, with her fists clenched. Alice was in a provocative mood and chattered away. I laughed but did not contribute. The Queen is her mother; Alice will always be forgiven. I cannot take quite the same liberties. I did not open the letter until I retired to bed at my actual home, a few days later, with the Schoens. And to my surprise – and disappointment – it was much more than a summons. The Queen was asserting her will.

"Bonetta," it began. "Your suitor, James Pinson Labulo Davies, will be in England on 15 May. I arranged for him to join us to dine at the castle. I think it would be good for you to interact once more. And I expect your presence at tea and to remain there until he joins us."

There was more. I ignored it and then I wrote a letter of my own.

133

My dearest Madam,

How thoughtful of you to arrange another opportunity that I might assess for myself once more the calibre of the man who appears to have chosen me. However, I have a prior engagement with Her Royal Highness, Princess Alice, and it would be impertinent for me to forgo that to entertain this incoming philanthropist. Certainly, there are spheres in which the will of a queen is the only one that matters. But when I am setting forth into the world, as I will be in attending this event with Her Royal Highness, known as I am as a ward of the Queen, my actions shall always reflect on the grace of Her Majesty. Were I to abruptly decline, when a space has been made for me, gowns prepared for me, food catered to me, a seatmate allocated for me, I would look ill-mannered. And if my experiences in this short life have thus far told me one thing, it is that those of my race cannot afford to take chances. Certainly not when they carry in their veins the reputation of the monarch, whose charity they dare not take for granted. As such, I will have to decline with regret, but I shall, I daresay, see Your Majesty for tea shortly, at the palace.

She would not be happy, but I was.

10 June 1861
Osborne House
Isle of Wight, England

For someone who has spent much of her life wandering through the Queen's castles, I confess I still found Edward's home, a Renaissance-era country manor, with its strong Palladian pillars in the smoothest sandstone, held a romantic appeal and inspired a wistful response. It was, to my mind, grander than all the palaces owned by the Queen's family, and not merely in size. Alice had brought me to his home, turning up in a brougham all her own. Wordlessly, she pulled me into the back with her. I stumbled in, a touch ungainly, and she sat before me looking dazzling, her hair in a braid around her head, set with emeralds, her dress bright like the breaking of dawn. She looked like a mythical creature; but for the tightness around her mouth, her small thin lips puckered in a crisp and nervous pout, she could be a faerie. But the light panic on her face was all too human.

"Mama received your letter, my dear," she said with a laugh, our little carriage clacking away towards Edward's house. "You are either the greatest genius or a complete and total fool. And were my father quite well I think he would declare you the love of his life. W-well, I think he would declare your mind a thing of genius. My mother might make you her greatest enemy."

"Your father is not well?"

Alice looked crestfallen.

I paused. How could I not know this? I thought about the Queen. Summoning me here, placing me. I felt controlled, powerless – it was patronizing. But I wonder, now, if that was her way of asserting *some* power *somewhere*. I know when I feel trapped in certain spaces, I try to manage others. I try to exert control over them instead. So I understand, now, her impetus then. At the time, however, I felt surprised that she had not told me about the state of Prince Albert. I felt resentful. I recall the look on Princess Alice's face; she wanted to divulge. But I was in no mood for second-hand insights. I glanced out of the window. We were heading onto some extraordinary land. And I did not think this was the kind of conversation that lends itself all that well to gathering at dinner. Thus I said gently, "I have no doubt Prince Albert shall recover."

"No, I actually doubt he will."

I did not know how to respond at first. Eventually, I said, "I doubt this provides much comfort, but I do know how it is to lose one's parents."

And she looked at me and said with characteristic frankness, "No, Bonetta, you do not, that is the thing. You do not know; you do not recall. I think that is somehow better…"

With anyone else I would have felt slighted, dismissed. But Alice was not wrong. I did not know the life that she spoke of. I had lost Captain Forbes in addition to my parents, but it seemed comparatively minor to what his actual children had felt, and they were still comparatively young to a seventeen-year-old Alice going off into a strange man's arms without even her father in another country to return to.

"I do not know what it is like," I agreed. "This is correct," and she turned to me in amazement.

"I cannot believe you said that."

"You are annoyed that I'm agreeing with you?"

"I am not annoyed. I am stunned because you are usually quite prickly. I had braced myself for some sort of pushback."

"As your father lies pale and unwell? I am not so bad, am I?"

"You are usually unmoved," she said with a merry and high laugh. I do not think she found it all that funny. But it was clear that this was the tone she wanted us to proceed in.

"Gallows humour was invented for a reason, was it not?"

"I think for those actually facing the gallows, though, not the mere spectators. Or those in proximity. The fortune hunter, the social climber—"

"I do not think we are those."

"Oh, I am not sure I can be."

"Ah yes. It does not get much higher than the Queen's daughter."

"Well. One could be queen," Alice offered.

"Oh, so, a little, but not much." I chuckled.

"One could be king."

"Well, no, because one is not male."

"Precisely. So it does get higher, but just out of reach."

"What on earth is this conversation?" I asked, and she fell about laughing.

The brougham had come to a stop. I glanced out through the carriage window at the expanse of vivid green that lay just beyond the pebbled stone of the courtyard entrance. The brougham had come as far as it could go; we would have to walk down a set of steps and along a short tree-lined path to the main doors. The coachman was standing outside the closed door, waiting for us to stop chattering away and appear ready to descend. I recall looking at him and then back at Alice, but I did not interrupt her.

"I told you. Prickly," she shot back, a smile on her face.

I did not *want* to interrupt her, even to descend the carriage and explore the beautiful gardens around us. "I am not!" I said, turning away from the coachman. "I just cannot follow how we ended up here talking about social climbers and then about monarchy and somehow about marriage and status."

"Well, yours will change once more, with this new groom."

"The African philanthropist?"

"Well, presumably?"

"No ... or not in a positive way. Not building upon 'Princess'. This title goes to the grave with me."

"Well, then, what are you getting out of the exchange?"

"Apparently, a rather handsome fortune. Marrying a rich man who shan't think of me as different or call me a— well, I suppose there is something."

"Well, I do not think of you as that. They are..." Alice paused. "Well, I do not really think of anyone as that. It is a quite horrible word."

I could only meet her eyes for a moment. Nobody had ever said that to me. "Do you really think so?"

"Of course, I was made to study Latin, you know."'

"'I do."

"Then you know. That word comes from '*necro*': death. You cannot call anybody that. Or rather, if you can, it certainly would not be because of their skin, but because of their character."

"You really think we could start calling s all kinds of people that name?"

"No. I think just banish the word altogether. One certainly could not call a whole group of people by the term; that is terrible."

There was a pause.

The coachman coughed outside. I opened the carriage door and allowed him to help me down the step on to the ground.

Princess Alice continued as though we were talking alone. "You are silent again. I thought you would be spiky on this topic."

I sighed. I knew best not to open my mouth. "Everybody has a view that insults everybody but me."

"Except for ones that insult you."

"Well, they would not dare say those things to my face."

"Yes, I suppose they would not."

"Although Annie, my foster sister, the daughter of the Schoens. She said some rather ghastly things."

"Ghastly?" Alice looked at me with glimmers of concern, but she also noted my chuckle.

"Yes." I took a deep breath but when I spoke my tone was light. "She spoke of putting me in a collar." Alice gasped. By this point, we had arrived. And before I could really catch my bearings, the doors had been opened. Instead of a whole flurry of staff and the hosts, only two footmen stood waiting.

From behind them, Edward stepped forward and I realized I had forgotten what he looked like. I could not remember the last time we saw each other. I realized I was staring at him and suddenly I found myself hoping it really was Edward because otherwise I was gazing impudently at a gentleman. That really would not do at all.

He bowed at Princess Alice.

"I do not know if you have had a chance to meet with Bonetta recently. But I daresay I recall you saw each other at St James's Palace." These are the first words I remember Alice saying to him. Perhaps it is fitting that I only recall those that concerned yours truly, but the mind works in mysterious ways that I shan't challenge today.

"I think we had a dance on that occasion as well." This was directed at me. His voice was low and smooth. It made me think of velvet. There was something dark and bright about it at the same time. His is a voice that feels independently alive. It was exciting. Even now, I recall that sensation. Was that brightness? It seemed so to me.

"Thank you for having us," I said. My tone was flat but, as I looked around a little, he smiled at me for a moment longer than a gentleman should.

We were late, I remember thinking, as all the other ladies had already retired to the drawing room. The housekeeper had stepped forward to take Princess Alice and me. It did surprise me that we would be separated from the men before dinner; I had not been to gatherings like this in too long. Or even at all. Balls and court functions, yes, but most of the social season remained a mystery to me.

"What a shame we cannot all be talking together," I said to Princess Alice, loudly enough that Edward overheard.

"They shall join us in the drawing room after dinner," Alice offered.

Turning back towards us, he smiled. "Well, you can join us in the smoking room after dinner, if you would prefer. Not at first, of course, but not too long after, either. We may not join you in the drawing room until very late. You may prefer to—"

"Smoke with the gentlemen?" Alice interjected, a look of theatrical shock on her face. Then smiled. "How could we refuse? Our last chance to be defiant princesses before a lifetime of husbands telling us how to behave!"

Edward's mouth twitched. I smiled. But really, I did not find it a funny prospect at all.

Was I now as betrothed as she? Does it still count as a betrothal if you do not wish to wed? But I kept the question in my head.

The Rose drawing room, a tall and handsome space with the merriment of women echoing off its crimson walls, was far too alive for my flattened mood. I counted ten ladies including the hostess, realizing that almost every other young lady was here with her mother. There would be two dining parties, two groups of twelve, I realized, wondering to myself if this were to be a night where women were expected to find suitors among the men who were presumably now in the smoking room.

At the time, I struggled to take it all in. One girl was playing the pianoforte with her mother's enthusiastic encouragement, but other girls were talking too loudly to hear it. Even with the windows open and the roaring fire, the cool spring air made its presence felt. I stared at the girls, fluttering like butterflies in their bright voluminous dresses, a bold and strangely daring vision in the dimmed light; the chandeliers hung low and loomed large, but offered light that remained strangely dull. The sky outside shimmered like a painting, the sunset had since slid in, while the sounds in the room were like monologues piled on top of one another. Words were spoken outwards but responses were not heard. Conversations were just each party waiting for the other to pause. Here and there, a couple of women seemed to lock eyes across the room. It was always mother and daughter. Or so it seemed.

I watched the exchanges, tucked in the first undisturbed corner of the room I could find. I wondered what shared understanding could be found within those glances. I suspect I shan't ever know.

Alice herself seemed a little listless, despite the flurry of people around her, and I was unable to perk up until we were all in the same room, dining together. I could not really hear what Edward was saying to his companions, and I had run out of things to say to my own. I stopped trying, staring into my goblet for most of the evening. Sometimes my eyes would look up and find his eyes across the loud and crowded room. Our gazes moved like smiles, greeting each other. I felt … it is impossible to say. But then at some point, Princess Alice declared she was restless and rose with the kind of imperiousness that only the Queen's daughter can do. Edward immediately followed suit, asserting it as his duty to entertain the needs of a daughter of a Queen, and asked her what she wished to do.

"I should like to explore that beautiful forest of yours," she said in truly decadent tones.

"Well, Princess Alice," I said, "I cannot leave you to venture into the forest alone."

"But I shall be with her," Edward gallantly responded.

"Well, then, I shall leave the two of you in peace to enjoy your sojourn," I insisted, but I smiled at him.

"Oh no," he said, "I think it would be unbecoming if we were to enter the forest unaccompanied. And I think you are the best person to accompany us." His mouth twitched as he spoke. I was attempting to rein in my own smile. Did anyone hear? Could they see? Was this provocative or just a fleeting bit of narrative in my head?

"I have never quite played the chaperone before, but I suppose there is a first for everything."

"Hardly. I think I am the chaperone for you two ladies, daughters of Her Majesty, by God and by birth. I daresay I have an obligation to make certain you navigate our forests with safety and satisfaction. It is growing dark, after all."

And before the conversation could coalesce into mere talk, he set about finding a valet and a lady's maid to provide us with some thick and marvellous coats to cover us as we departed.

We ventured out with a purposeful step. Edward was keen to take us into the forests, as per Princess Alice's request, while I was too busy taking in the acres of unspoilt green as we wandered through to think much of the final destination at all. The long grass was lush yet placid, smooth and pliant as our boots sank into the soft belly of the land, but the forests I could see grew no closer all the while. Our strides became a leisurely amble; eventually we meandered and Princess Alice began to feel tired. "I think I need to head back."

We all should, I almost said. Instead the words I spoke were, "Let us walk you back."

Edward agreed, "Yes, we shall."

There seemed no conversation necessary to confirm that he and I would return to the forest. The air was cool and calm as the darkness descended upon us, and under our feet crunched the loose twigs of the undergrowth. As we made our way unsteadily through thickets we found ourselves before a wall and, without hesitation, I clambered onto the bench before me and stood with my hands along the top of it, looking out at an array of untouched fields, acres of unspoiled beauty. We must have stood and watched for hours, as under the deepening night those endless spheres of green began to turn a radiant vivid blue.

Behind us, our matching footprints left a candid trail, illuminating our trip.

I stared at them; I felt exposed, and he turned to follow my gaze.

"I shall carry you back," he whispered, as though in response to a question that the air had asked.

I looked at him, but his eyes were still facing the way in which we came.

"I shall carry you back, and there will only be one set of footsteps that return. So they will have to wonder where we went, what took place and maybe even who we really are. There will be nothing and no way to enlighten them, even if they came and stood right here."

I stared at him, my lips parting as I tried to bring myself to speak. His eyes found mine and then he swept me off the bench and strode all the way into the castle, carrying me in his arms. A lone pair of footprints making their way through the faltering dark. And the trees kept our secrets in their hearts.

11 June 1861
The Rectory, Palm Cottage
Gillingham, England

I am certain that were this to be any other young woman's life, that such a momentous evening would be quite enough to be left to think about. But not for nothing am I Sarah Forbes Bonetta, who must recount such moments a whole month after they happen, so little time has been granted to think to herself in the days between! What was this experience I found myself in? Had *I*, among a sea of ladies and their mothers scanning the eligibility of their dining partners, found by sheer and total accident that I might be falling in love? Falling into something, and certainly of the romantic kind. This is the kind of moment a girl swoons for. Not the formal fittings as she prepares her wedding gown or the procession as she sweeps through the church followed by babes with fists of flowers to make solemn vows to secure one's property or safety in marriage before some crinkly old vicar. Does one not dream of nights that run on into the very next day? Moments alone where you might lose your footing, but never your reputation? Gentlemen who might make you feel...

Well, I look back a month later with sympathy, if not shame, at how yearning and ardent my heart was. Under the haughty façade was I a mere hapless romantic like Elizabeth Schoen? I was not, and remain quite stoic. I am capable of being enthralled, as it were, but I knew all too well the complications it could lead to and was altogether unenthused about the freedoms any kind of married love might offer me. I was a princess with a queen's resources behind me. I should not *need* a marriage. Which is not to say I would never feel love. But I am an African girl in Victorian England. Who was I expecting would feel love for me?

I did not find any way to raise the question as Edward and I made our way back towards the house. I had no way to tell the time, but I knew dawn had not broken and midnight had passed. By the time we grew close I was thankfully on my feet again, in an unspoken recognition of the need to be discreet. The entrance hall was empty, it appeared, and as we gingerly began to head towards different quarters, I wondering how I might even find out where Princess Alice was sleeping, a young footman clattered loudly into view, all but announcing our arrival.

"Michael!" Edward snapped. "Are you aware of the time?"

The footman, Michael, who stood a foot taller than Edward, went red. "My lord," he coughed, and then, to my surprise, he looked at me.

Edward straightened up and glanced at him as if to suggest *he knew better than to question a lady's behaviour*, and I marvelled at how hierarchy works in practice. It was the early hours of the day and we had walked in together, probably looking rather dishevelled. Michael would be wrong to draw adverse conclusions, but not unreasonably so.

Michael went, if possible, redder. "Um ... Miss Forbes Bonetta?"

"Yes," I said, in a tone I hoped equalled Edward's imperious one.

"There is a member of Her Majesty's court waiting with a carriage for you."

I spluttered. Not the most ladylike response, I admit.

"What madness is this? A jest, Michael, at this time of night?"

"No ... no. Her Royal Highness is in the carriage already. They are both waiting with a coachman. The carriage arrived some hours ago. I suggest you go and meet them."

"Do you, Michael? Is this your advice?" Edward's tone was dripping with sarcasm.

I knew not where he got the confidence. I wished to sink into the ground and disappear.

"Michael," I said quickly, "please find me a lady's maid and have her escort me to where Princess Alice is waiting with the courtier so we can return to ... the palace?"

"Windsor Castle, I believe, is where they will be taking you, Miss Forbes Bonetta."

"Yes, fine. Please find that lady's maid. Edward will join you. And I am not 'Miss Forbes', I am Princess Bonetta."

Michael looked nervously at Edward. "Yes, Princess," he muttered and hurried away.

Edward paused to look back at me. He mouthed words I cannot remember and then he too left.

I was escorted to a different entrance by a young lady's maid. I told her I had become lost trying to return to the smoking room and fell asleep in one of the morning rooms. She concurred with politeness and asked no questions. I mentioned that Michael had found me and it did not seem proper to escort me to Princess Alice unchaperoned, and thus I was very grateful for her discreet acquaintance.

She smiled when I said that and added, "I can keep your confidences very well, Princess."

I wanted to tell her that 'Miss Bonetta' was fine. Instead I asked her, "Is Princess Alice alone?"

"She is with a palace courtier..." The maid trailed off.

"What can you tell me about him?"

She looked at me and continued walking through the halls in silence.

Frowning, I stopped.

Sighing, she turned to me and said, "I think he is somebody you only wish to meet this once."

"What does that mean?"

"Trouble."

"Trouble? *I* am in trouble, is this what you mean to say?"

"I said neither that nor anything else." The lady's maid hurried but, at the entrance hall, pivoted and entered into a function room. *Another* drawing room, if I recall. And so far from the others. I remember thinking the house had not been designed efficiently.

"I thought Alice was in the carriage..." I trailed off as the maid entered the drawing room, curtsied to the occupants and left without a word. I realized then that she did not tell me her name.

I had not asked.

"It's *Her Royal Highness Princess* Alice to you, Miss Forbes Bonetta." A crisp voice cut through my thoughts. "I hope you do not instruct servants everywhere to drop the formal address and royal title of the daughter of Her Majesty the Queen."

It was clearly the 'palace courtier', whose name and role continue to elude me a month after that encounter. He was lean and thin with a pinched face and he stood upright while Alice slouched in silence on a nearby chaise. His hair gleamed as if it had been smoothly pressed with oil, and even his moustache seemed oiled into obedience. Grey eyes blank of anything but flat condemnation, it was hard to read any status from his manner. I can never distinguish one courtier's attire from another. But the entitlement of his forthright tone would have told me he was of senior rank even if Alice's sullen demeanour had not announced it already.

I stood in silence looking from one person to the other.

When it became clear I would not break the silence, he began.

"Her Majesty has sent a carriage. You are to return to Windsor Castle at once."

I did not speak.

"I am aware it is late," he added, as though speaking over a voiced objection on my part. "It is very late. But you were not easy to find."

"It is not quite a castle, but it is still rather a large country house."

"With acres of land."

I ignored his pointed comment. But I noted how much personality he was apparently free to demonstrate. If nothing else it was, at least enough for me, to reduce the presence of mine. "We should be on our way, then? I trust it would not be prudent to keep the Queen waiting."

Without a word the courtier rang a bell and Michael arrived with another footman, all our belongings included. "Please put our things in the carriages," the courtier instructed him. Michael nodded and both the footmen headed outside. Quite why, given all the time they had spent waiting, this had not been done before, I could not fathom.

"Rise, *Your Royal Highness*," the courtier said and turned to me as though to include me wordlessly in the instruction.

Alice was sluggish as she stumbled to her feet. The courtier marched ahead of us towards the carriages waiting outside. For a few horrible moments, I thought he was going to enter the carriage and sit with us. But apparently not. He sent us into the first carriage, and as I climbed in after Alice I could not help but look back to see him making his way into his own car.

I let out an audible sigh. "Who is that?"

"Who?" Alice asked, the colour back in her cheeks now that the courtier had left our midst.

"Him, the—"

"The Palace Dispatch? Ladies and gentleman," she intoned, "you just made the acquaintance of..." *Perhaps I willed myself to forget.*

"He is French?"

"His father was and, well..." Alice laughed, her voice dropping. "We are all a bit foreign in the Royal Family, are we not? And I daresay we like our foreign blood. We like foreigners in general." She gave me a knowing smile.

"Oh really?"

"We-ell, not disobedient ones. No. Not disobedient ones."

"And by golly, we were."

"We?" Alice burst out laughing. I shall never forget how her laughter sounded. "No, Bonetta, *you* were, and since I was the temptation who led you through the valley of the shadow of death, Mama shall seek *my* head!"

"You sound rather excited."

"It seems fitting for the moment!"

"Worry might better suit the mood."

"You want me to be worried?"

"Only if you seek advice on your deportment."

"For which I need *your* help?"

I put two fingers on each side of my neck. "It is only your head at risk, is it not? Mine is quite secure."

The carriage lurched suddenly over a pothole and Alice looked at me, her rakish grin in place. "How certain are you of this?"

"How angry will she be?" I asked her suddenly. Looking back I cannot recall what jolted the change in mood. One moment I was laughing along with Alice and the next thinking about meeting my fate at Windsor Castle.

Alice matched my sober tone for once. "Honestly, Bon, I am curious as to what will happen. Truly. When am I ever in trouble? I always do what I am supposed to. In fact, I do more than I should. She has castles of servants, but who nursed *her* mother when she was sick? Who has been nursing Papa? Who takes care of her menagerie of children? Who let her choose their spouse? Me. I am never appreciated for being the royal nursemaid, and so I suspect listening to her unleash her temper will make a pleasant change. It can hardly last. Within a week she will have some sorry task she does not trust the servants with and cannot get the family to assist on. Who would she need? Me. It is harder to extract favours from those at whom you are shouting at length. Do not concern yourself. She is far fonder of you than she is any of us and she would not tell you off. I think she grows more brutal as Papa grows more frail."

Frail? I did not ask, but I could hear the word echoing in my head. It carried a level of severity I felt unprepared for. Had he really been this sick? She had attempted to tell me in the carriage down, but it seemed inappropriate and I felt voyeuristic. Why did I need to revel in this after all, when he would soon recover?

While I ruminated in my head, Alice was fretting aloud. I forced myself to listen.

"I think that she ... I think that this ... I think that a wedding is..." Can I remember exactly how she stuttered out her sentences? Not precisely. But there was a lot of anxious mumbling which equated to her stating that with Prince Albert so sick, a wedding seemed inappropriate at best.

I did not know what my role was here. I had never before had a peer who wanted to confide in me with such anxieties. There is nothing a spectator can do. I could not improve Prince Albert's health; I could not pretend a wedding made any difference to whether he was dying or not. As to her implication that a celebration was ghoulish at this point, I could conceive of no answer. I lacked even her own ability to be arch and funny, to evoke the humour of the gallows, to make us laugh at our bleak scenarios.

I tried out a phrase in my head as she burbled along. *Excuse my limited sympathy, Alice; my own father is already dead.* No. It sounded like a condemnation. She would not realize it was my feeble attempt at wit. Such was my inward spiral about how to be of use that I failed to follow her thoughts, and by the time I regained the thread of the conversation, or her monologue, it had turned into a set of complaints about her mother.

"... I do not understand why she is always demanding I do everything, clinging to me and even requiring me to do..." There was a sharp intake of breath and I looked up, but Alice did not finish the thread. After a pause she added, "And yet also shepherding me into a marriage when she is not ready to let me go. I would rather be elsewhere than saddled with all the grief and work of caring for everyone here but..." And I forget the exact words she used. But the sentiment was clear.

"It is a great honour that you have chosen to meet me, dear Bonetta." His voice, though gently mocking, seemed more pointed than I found acceptable. I did not answer. We had sat through a stilted tea and were back taking a tour of the grounds. I did not really know what I might show him, and in truth I was not inclined to make an effort.

"I rather thought I was being foisted upon you. My presence, a touch unwelcome. And thus, I am charmed to note that you wish to see me again."

"Well, now that we are here perhaps we need not belabour that point."

"Oh? A sore spot. Your interest?" His smile was ... well, I was charmed. It held a charm. I shan't say it was winning. It was slightly too annoying for that. But it was ... well, it was a smile. Who does not like a smile?

"It is nice to see you smile," he said.

"I was not smiling. In fact, you were smiling!" My voice rose with indignation.

He laughed at me.

"You laughed at me."

"You were amusing."

"Like a child?" I demanded.

"I think in that one instance, yes."

I was stymied for a moment. "You put that so tactfully..."

"Well, yes, because I do not see you as a child usually."

Hmm.

"I am serious. And this is something to note about my manner: I do not patronize. I do not pander or coddle. I do not bother to be tactful. Because I trust you are adult enough to handle the truth. I would pretend if I were to present you with a façade of myself. But I have little intention of doing that. I am so often subject to people's *misrepresentations.*" He sighed. "While it may be prudent to construct a pleasing form of myself, it seems more practical, but also more peaceful, to simply show up precisely as I am."

It was not the kind of comment to which one would offer a sharp retort, and I was also unwilling to see it dismissed. This might have been the first interesting thing he had said. Which does not mean I needed to marry him at once. If a man is only expected to make one interesting comment every few encounters, well, what kind of marriage are we sending women off to? But he took my silence for the positive it was, and then it was his turn to smile.

"Well," I said, and I did not need to say more. And his smile grew wider. I enjoyed it. But still, I was largely bored. Perhaps because we had the chaperone shuffling quietly behind us. An English woman. There was little that could be said frankly as a result of her presence. There were things I might want to ask, a sense of himself I would hope to explore, in a manner that a chaperone from England would struggle to understand. Hampered by an audience as we were, unable to ask my questions, my interest began to wane. The best way I have found to endure tiresome interactions that one cannot quickly escape from is to ask questions, limited in scope, but also great many of them. Because questions do not require you to continue the thread of the conversation. They do not even require you to pay all that much attention. People love to talk. It is never difficult.

I did not want to do that with James, but it seemed I was going to have to, with the chaperone behind me. I felt a slight frustrated pity that he thought my interest might actually be sincere, but had the overall sense that I was somehow bound to this man anyway. This was perhaps what made the situation something of a travesty in the first place: James was an interesting man. He was dashing, handsome, bold in a new way and a little daring. I should have liked to verbally spar with him some more and, in the absence of others, to unpack what he was like. But there was no room to and, for the Queen, there was no reason to. He could have had the personality of stone. He could have been the brutish man English stereotypes imply. The fact that he had money and a Nigerian connection meant that I would have been shipped off to him all the same. In the future, he will tell our great grandchildren while I scrub away on some floor about how I was a present to the Queen and later *from* the Queen. Even to my future descendants I will forever be the gift and thus the gaud. Bonetta, the bestowal ... for ever.

I suspect a little of my pensiveness began to unfold on my face, for he turned to me and said, "Bonetta, Etta, it is getting a touch chilly. I think I am honour-bound to return you to Her Majesty, the Queen, your protector, and take my leave for the day. Perhaps we might discuss with each other again. I am enjoying these conversations."

This time my smile was an unbridled expression of relief. He looked taken aback and, quite frankly, I could hardly explain. I did find that I wanted to. And as much as I was dispassionate about him as a suitor for me, a small part of me was indignant on his behalf as well. I knew that he had chosen me himself, but I rather wish he somehow had insight into my lack of interest. And the reasons why. I suspect he might have made a greater effort to reveal his character, so we might get along in spite of what others might think about our connection. But he did not, and I did not, and I let him guide us back to the castle. I noticed with amusement his familiarity with the navigation.

"Have you been here other times I have yet to know about?"

I found myself asking with a smile. "You seem to remember the way so well."

"Well, no, but I commandeered a ship. I was a sailor before I was a philanthropist. Grasping directions is part of my natural skill set."

"Ah yes. You are a seaman, a seafarer – a wayfarer, even."

"Yes."

I wanted to make a joke, but I found I was a touch intrigued. "Do you miss it?"

"Do I miss the seas? Do you?"

"I had a terrible time when I was a child. I was not in control. You would have been in control."

"Would I? Do you really think I would have been in control?"

"But you were the captain of a ship."

"I was. I had some control, some relative measure."

"Do you miss that?

"Oh, I have much more of it now."

"Not in this country."

He looked at me. He looked at the chaperone, but it was not clear what she had heard, although she was watching. "No. Of that you are correct," he said. "Nor you."

"Well, I have more here. I have more, that much more—"

"Than I?" he asked, and his eyes flashed. Briefly, but they flashed.

"—than I did on the ship," I said with a pointed frown.

He looked apologetic. But he looked back at the chaperone and so did I. And we both knew he could not really apologize. Did he really think that I was attempting to lord my superior capacity to navigate a country that thinks quite poorly of black people over him? To hail the greater permissions I was granted over him or others with less? I tried to look past the deep insults at the centre of that miscommunication. What good would it do to hold it against him? And yet I could not let it go somehow. We walked through the entrance talking about this and that.

Then at the end he raised my hand to his mouth – not to kiss it, but to actually bow to it.

"I would not do that," I said, and he looked up at me and looked at my hand. I chuckled. "Ah, more miscommunication." I shook my head. "When I said what I said earlier, I really meant that my time on the ship made me feel more powerless."

He nodded slowly.

"I believe you."

"I would never ... it would not be fair of me. I am not naive. I put no stock in the freedom that I have to move in this country. I know ... what this place is, who I am." I whispered the last part and he nodded at me.

Looking back I wonder if he believed me, because *I* do not believe me. I simplified that which I meant but is ultimately quite untrue. I could not list the number of things that I enjoy about my life that I would not yield, and they all connect very closely with the permission, or the privilege, I am granted by my proximity to power. I have access to many things that most people, Englishmen, slaves or otherwise, do not. And I wished to keep the access I enjoyed. I would not give it up for anything. I know what kind of fate awaits me without it.

"The world is a complex place, Bonetta, Etta," and he leaned over and kissed me on the forehead. It felt like a memory being imprinted. I did not dare touch my forehead and resolved never to wash it again.

I still did not wish to marry him soon. But I had high hopes for us enjoying our time together. It was only just beginning, after all. It was new.

Depending on who you ask, I did misjudge. I did make the wrong choice. Not by any specific action but by what I set in motion by seeking James out once more. I had found myself having a better time than I had expected. And so I allowed it to be known that I might be available to meet with him again. I had intended to reconvene first with the Queen, but she was so thrilled by this development, and I was so thrilled by her joy, that I basked in that halcyon glow rather than apply strategic thought. It appears I do have a weakness for the approval of others.

15 June 1861
The Rectory, Palm Cottage
Gillingham, England

And so we met once more. He joined me in the library.

So much for tea.

We did first sit in a drawing room but, feeling stifled, we went into one of the old libraries. I wanted to show him some of my favourite books. The chaperone was at one end of the library. And I urged him to join me, but discreetly; we could not hurry, lest we catch her attention and have her come and find us. But we could amble quietly. I think she had been misled by the academia of a library and did not realize that there were so many nooks and crannies, and it would not be prudent for her to leave us to ourselves.

Needless to say, nothing unbecoming of a princess took place there. Neither his position nor mine would ever allow us to take such risks. I traced my fingers along the bookshelves where I thought a particular text would be, that I was hoping he would find. I did not tell him the name because I wanted the impact to be greater. But before I could get much further, he stopped and drew my attention to a book. "Forbes?" he said, reading the spine. "Is this related to your guardians?"

"I suspect so, if it is of Clan Forbes." I walked over to him and, taking the book, I glanced at the cover. My heart began racing.

I was on it. The cover. It was me.

The cover was one of the early portraits I did soon after we descended from the ship and soon after the Queen had agreed to be my ward. I looked smaller, vulnerable and deeply unhappy. I do not think I had seen that photograph for years. I certainly did not know it was printed on the cover of a book that purports to talk about me without my consent or awareness, nor that the finished product was here in one of the Queen's libraries. I did not say any of this to James. Not that he was looking at me. He was thumbing through the book.

"You wrote this together?"

I did not answer. I could not.

There was so long a silence that after a while he began to look confused. He glanced up at me and then back at the page. As if goaded by his gaze, I started to speak.

"Well, if you look at the photo, I was too young to have anything of a narrative ... any narrative skill to offer." The words stumbled out, my attempt at an indulgent tone stymied by my own incoherence. "You flatter me with the idea that I could then have been a worthy contributor to my own tale. I was a babe in arms, back then! I might at this point have some useful reflections, but certainly not when this was written."

"Ah yes," he said, absently, returning to the pages, "it makes sense. I do not think I see your voice in this at all; it is very much the gaze of a stranger."

I could not say anything else.

"This was your guardian. Did he interview you?"

"No."

"Why not?"

"I suspect he thought it would be traumatic, given what I endured."

"So he wrote *about* you instead."

"Well, he kept a journal anyway, he always did. He was a seaman. Keeping journals is pretty commonplace. You will know this. And this was such an unusual experience. And he had also been taking me to the Queen; he needed to keep account of what had taken place." *And, and, and ...* I wanted to shudder at the sound of my own voice.

There is something sickening about having to defend a position you do not believe, but I felt that while it was one thing for me to be angry at Forbes, it was entirely another for a stranger to come in with all of the assumptions that I could see illuminating James's face, and start besmirching my guardian's memory. Forbes was, without question, a truly great man. It was not fair to let his good name be attacked when he was not able to defend himself. And thus, like the good daughter I am, I took it upon myself to do so. But I was angry at Forbes, at the position I was placed in, at the sense of shame his actions evoked in me, at the audacity at having to defend him in lieu of expressing myself. Maybe I was supposed to feel angry. There did not seem to be any other way to process what was taking place.

"He used you," said James.

I had struggled through the realizations myself too recently to be too quick to deflect. "This is one interpretation I expect," was my only reply. And he looked at me with incredulity.

He said, "I could not live in a country where I was such a spectacle for others."

"Well, you have never had to."

"Oh, I have had to, but then I left. As soon as I could, I left."

"It is not so simple for everyone," I said.

"Of course," and his gaze softened. "But you are marrying me, and I have the resources to take you anywhere. And we will go where you will not be tolerated or indulged, nor subject to some superior gaze, but where you are above the gaze, where you will never be seen as anything but the descendant of monarchs."

But I was marrying him, he had casually asserted. He had taken it as a foregone conclusion.

Unbidden, I felt something prickling under my skin. "I am not aware that your betrothal has been accepted," I spoke, in a tone so lofty I surprised myself.

He opened his mouth several times and then stopped.

"It is interesting that this is the response that you have to all that I said."

"Why is it interesting?"

"Well, you do not engage with whether or not you want to go away, or if you wish to remain here." As he spoke, he looked awkwardly through the bookshelves to see where the chaperone might be. "You just focus on whether you have to be married off to me."

"Really? Did I use any of those words?"

"You did not need to—"

"I do not see why the idea of not wanting to be passive in my own life is such an affront to you by design."

"You seem quite passive in your own life right here," he said, brandishing the book at me.

"I was a child, " I snarled, "and an orphan in a foreign land!" *How dare you!*

"Well, you have also returned," he shot back. "You *were* in Sierra Leone."

"What is your point?"

"My point is that you clearly wished to be back here."

Tensely, I replied, "I wished to be far from the man, the king, who had ordered my sacrifice."

"He was not in Sierra Leone."

"He was not *far* from Sierra Leone either."

James was silent, disdain furrowing his brow.

I did not want to hear whatever he might say next. Loudly I stated, "I wished to be among people who are powerful enough to keep him from me altogether."

"As I said, I have the means."

"Everybody has promises." The disdain dripped from my tongue. "Do you not suppose that my original parents *promised* to stand by me? Do you think they told me they and everyone else in my family would be dead, and I would be a possession or plaything for the world's richest rulers? They did not. They had no idea this would be their fate and mine. You have money today. How nice. Even if that was a sufficient answer, I am not seeking that as a solution. To be within reach of the kingdom where I was almost sacrificed because I have the money to ensure he does not try again is to lack ambition or just hope for one's own existence. And as to the promised fortune, well ... I would not have that money. It would be yours and thus my safety, my access to it, my resources would be contingent on you. *You* would have the money. And I should strive to be in proximity to such a people again? Let us not pretend that is a smart plan. You can see why leaving Sierra Leone and finding somewhere where I have more control over my life, including the fact that I get one, was thus a prudent choice for me—"

James cut me off. "To live with these people who treat you as a gift, a gaud, a spectacle ... how much better is that than subjugation by him?

There, you were a person so significant you had to be a sacrifice to the gods. Here, you are an item. So significant they want to put you on the shelf, put you in a brooch, pin you on a blouse ... and you want to play ornament because it means you get to stay alive. I hear that, but let us not pretend that to be an ornament is more virtuous."

"A virtuous life is a fanciful idea for those with agency over their lives right now. For me—"

"If it is about survival, acknowledge that this is subpar survival, and that your options are limited."

Why? "I have no reason to subscribe to your narrative. You are not some egalitarian crusader; you want to marry me because I descend from a monarchy. You are a man with money, who had a career in the military and on the seas. I am a princess. Therein lies my currency for you. So do not pretend we are not all somewhat dazzled by hierarchies, titles and elitism."

"Nobody said we are not."

"You implied that I was enamoured by the chance to be an ornament for an Englishman as opposed to being a dead body for an African king."

His eyes flashed again. "You are simply being hyperbolic."

"No, I am spelling out what you only dared hint."

He laughed mirthlessly. "All this? Because you cannot say no to a proposal?"

"One cannot say no in response when no question has been asked!

170

All this because you cannot ask, you must state. That does not bode well for any kind of marriage, where you do not discuss, you simply assert your authority. I have grown tired of others asserting their authority over my person. I would like to assert some authority of my own."

He was speechless. I could hear the clacking feet of the chaperone, heaving down the aisles.

James turned briefly and looked back at me. "You may have a short window of time in which to do that. How would you like to demonstrate your autonomy, at this very moment?"

"By telling you that I shall not be marrying you. There has been no proposal, and to the extent that there has been one I do not accept. I do not agree. Not to a written proposal, not to an assumption thrown in as an aside. I am not seeking a caretaker or a guardian. My life will not be buffeted around indefinitely, according to the whims of whoever wants to have me as a brooch on their blouse or an ornament on their shelf. That is what I will say. I am not marrying you, you did not ask me, *I do not want to*, and I did not enjoy this conversation."

The Queen chastised me. It was an ugly moment. It is quite unbecoming to be on the receiving end of the displeasure of not one but two people in a single day, and I confess I was tired of it by the end of her speech. We had had so candid a conversation before and so recently,

I could not fathom the chilling nature of her indifference.

Of course, I could not tell her the deeper nature of my conversation with James. I daresay she may not have wished me to marry him herself if she had heard it; more importantly, he could be socially ostracised or experience some pernicious hardship I cannot now imagine. So I simply stood and endured her frustration that an open and clear proposal or 'recognition of the fact' was met with such derision by myself.

She sent me back to the Schoens. I confess I have never been dismissed by her really; our time together would usually come to a natural conclusion, or there was a planned time at which a brougham would come and pick me up. But to be sent from her presence was unfamiliar – and painful; I felt the sting of indignation.

23 June 1861
The Rectory, Palm Cottage
Gillingham, England

I received a letter from Alice. It was about a week later. It was full of her profuse sympathies. She also wanted insights, it appeared, into the situation with James, and she mentioned that Edward had hoped to hear from me and had asked for my permission to grant him an address at which to write to me. I shuddered at the idea of him discovering the Schoens' address, were he to send letters out and then perhaps, one idle day, take a horse and a long, long route and find himself at their comparatively ramshackle rectory with their barefoot children and their dirty mouths. I just ... it felt too much.

Would it bother you terribly? I asked, in my last to Alice, *if I were to use* your *address for correspondence – perhaps 'For the attention of Sarah Forbes Bonetta'? Would that be something you would be willing to help me with?*

It was rhetorical, because I knew Princess Alice would say yes. Who would not want to do this? Be the handler of love notes and the facilitator of secret intimacies. Perhaps I get ahead of myself when I say love notes.

I did not know that I wished to send Edward a love note. I certainly hoped that perhaps he might feel that he heard or received a love note when I spoke my words. I am not sure why, or from where the fixation had arisen. Sometimes I think it is just the tiredness from a lack of compassion. Feeling overburdened, underheard, underserved – and that he was seeking communication added a little something to my sense of self-worth. I wanted to write to him. I wanted to meet. I wanted to be seen.

We graduated from secret letters. It was Princess Alice who made it possible. As I suspected, she was so bored that she was eager to help with a little rendezvous. Edward's home was in Surrey Hills, and Windsor Castle was comparatively close by. The plan was pleasingly simple: I would visit Alice at Windsor and have one of their broughams take me to Edward's estate. A lifetime of serving the monarchy meant that their coachmen could be trusted to be discreet. Or so Alice assured me. We tried it one day early in June.

His carriage met mine on the very outskirts of the grounds.

"Bonetta." It was the first word on his lips as I arrived. Edward opened the carriage door and my name tumbled out of his mouth. He helped me down the steps. I did not look at the carriage driver. He did not look at me. There was no chaperone. But it was daytime. We walked through fields. We walked in silence, our feet squelching on the wet grass. I was reminded of that morning, that dawn. The soft patter of his feet on the dew. My legs were in his arms. It felt like we were entering a new day, together, entering a new moment.

Today did not feel so different. It was inching towards summer. The sun was bright but tentative. It felt like my soul. We walked with our hands in an identical pose, locked together behind our back. We did not dare walk too closely to each other and, as we marched through this open field, my shoes were not the best for this. I could not have worn more fitting ones lest I draw attention to the possibility of an alternative plan to the one I conveyed when I departed from Windsor. And thus we squelched through the mud. My shoes, with their noisy, squishing steps, made up for the lack of conversation. His words were awkward: he kept attempting to start a conversation, but it was all so oddly disjointed. I was barely able to reply to anything that he said. I had, of course, this betrothal sitting on my chest. The weight of all the anger it evoked that I was never able to speak to, that no one allowed me to express...

"Bonetta—"

"Edward, I am engaged," I burst out, and he looked at me. He went slightly red. "It is not my choice. Nothing is ever my choice. I do not know what annoys me more: a proposal I do not wish to accept, or the foregone conclusion that I must."

"You must not." Edward stopped and turned to face me. The sky was harder to see now. We had entered the first of many forests.

The trees stretched up and formed a little cabin around us, branches interlocked overhead. The hesitant sun barely getting a peek in, there was hardly a ray of light to illuminate the clearing.

But he was looking straight into my eyes. His, green, like the colour of freshly cut grass, were vivid yet slightly wet. Almond-shaped with long lashes. So thick and curled, they seemed more feminine than mine. His was a face of beauty, of bashfulness. I wondered whether on an English girl it might be a face I envied.

I wondered what he saw when he looked at me, at my almond eyes that went up at the top and up at the side, whereas his slipped into the half-moon crescent in the opposite direction.

"You mustn't ... you mustn't accept it."

It was only later that I would find that statement rather less romantic than I did in the moment. Later, my need for autonomy would push back against the automatic instruction to do something else, according to someone else. But at the time I did not hear it for what it was. A young man telling me that I could not marry someone else. I did not want to presume. But I looked at him and waited. Even the most reserved person will talk their way out of an inadvertent silence.

And he gabbled into the air, "You mustn't. I should not ask or tell, but I insist. You do not belong with him because you belong with me. *You belong with me.*" It was said with a burst of confidence. It sounded certain. Like he knew.

I opened my mouth and he kissed me. It was all too much to take in. Soft hands. Against the curve of my cheek. His lips pressed to mine. Soft. Wet. Rushed. Swift – it was an urgent, ardent moment. I felt a pressure; I wanted to pull him closer, but I am still the protégée of the Queen, a Princess. I am a woman of honour. He stepped back. He looked at me and I looked at him. We did not say anything. He paused, moving more slowly now, as if to confirm my silence was my 'yes'. And he kissed me again, much more slowly this time. The kiss of one who knows the best ones last.

A soft brush against my lips. This time his hand held the base of my throat. My pulse raced against his palm. Time seemed to stop, to swirl and swell around us. When I think back to that day, the next memory I have is back at the Schoens. I could not tell how I returned to Windsor, what I said or did not say to Princess Alice. But once I had returned home, the house was ringing with the news of my betrothal to James. The Schoens were ecstatic. I wondered at which point the offer had turned to an acceptance. I wondered with amusement how thrilled they would feel if they knew I had spent the afternoon kissing another man while they insisted I was marrying this one. There was something about this audience of people asserting facts about my life that I did not agree with; suddenly, those facts could become my life and I would be married off. I retired to my room, heaving myself up to the top floor, pushing my bedroom door ajar to sit in a heap. I wrenched off my taffeta gown and thrust it onto the ground near my feet.

Annie appeared somehow. I was unpleasantly surprised. I had no room for mind games today. "Can I help you, Annie?"

"Oh," she replied, her voice vague, "I was just coming to congratulate you. On your ... your upcoming nuptials."

"Thank you." I spoke in a toneless voice hoping she would go away.

She did not. She stood there, nervous. Also smiling. "Sarah ... I just had a thought. That all your education, your French, your fluency, all of that is all going to be wasted when you marry this brute."

On a different day I might have put her in her place. I would have pointed out the hypocrisy of her own racist agenda. Pointed to the evidence of how unfair the world is and how this impacts those with less power or privilege than her. But I was tired. It was a long, long, long day. It felt like a long life.

So I said, "Well, if he is a brute, he is still the only person to understand me and where I'm from. Perhaps I am a brute just like him."

And then something unexpected happened. Almost silent. I could hear her foot tapping on the floor. Then much too loudly she spoke.

"I should never have done that."

Inwardly, I felt my shoulders sink.

"It was so close to your birthday, as well. I was mean. I have been jealous. You get all the attention." The words came thick and fast, loud emotionless statements that I did not know what to do with. I kept staring at the floor. "You look so different, and all my life I was told how wonderful you are: the higher class you are from, your education, your manners, all the languages. I was taught to admire. Maybe they feared I would not respect you, because of your race. But for all our Christian piety, I only learned how to envy. Nobody taught me how to be your friend. Nobody ever said I should."

"Perhaps they assumed friendship need not be taught." My tone was flat and I did not look up. Does 'friendship' need to be taught? Does one have to be told? Memories from my time in Freetown rose to the top of my mind. Hordes of well-mannered, mal-intentioned girls. Cruel in the dark but presentable in public. Perhaps friendliness does have to be taught. Before Princess Alice, who was I friendly towards? Who were my friends?

"I am so sorry." She repeated the sentiment a few times. Again, she spoke a little too loudly and looked outwards, not in any way at me. I did not want her to look me in the eyes. I did not want to have to deal with the emotions of that whole exchange, my history with her at the Schoens, now, just because she wanted to.

"It was a year ago," was all I could say.

"I know! I am so late—"

Oh God. I put my head in my hands. *Make it stop!*

What happened to ice-cool Annie, who had been apparently seething with envy. Could we not bring back even a modicum of her reserve?

She actually grew silent for some time. And then, as if debating, she joined me on the floor. Were I less tired I might have asked her not to. But I just let it happen. She sighed and said, "I do not want to get married. I look at you, how you are written about in society magazines, and you have this patronage, this education and these opportunities. I ... well, I am very admiring. And, quite frankly, I often think I would much rather have your life than mine. You are special – you do know that?"

It was not the first time I had heard this. It was something I had heard many times before. Always said with a similar level of vagueness, whereby I did not really know what was meant beyond that I was an African born into power, in a world where Africans are powerless or it is believed they should be.

In any case, Annie continued, "You are special because you are the protégée of the Queen, because you are written about more than her own daughters. That is a currency that nobody else has. You are known all around the world. For you to give that up ... to be married? You cannot give up something so valuable. Do not give up the Queen!"

And what if the Queen is trying to give me up herself? I did not ask aloud.

"I would love to have your life," Annie carried on. She sounded dreamy. Almost delirious. Almost.

"Would you, really?" My voice was low. *So envy was behind your years of bitter cruelty towards me?* But I knew better than to remind her of that out loud. "Would you trade any one of your family members, or all of the Schoens, for some gold in a far-flung country that would usually consider you under its foot?" *Would you be like me?* I wanted to add. I doubted she would choose to.

I did not need to look up to know her face was flushed.

I raised my head in the end, lest I seem too judgmental. But I could not muster any real empathy. I stared at her but my expression was blank. "Do not think that there is *anything* for which you would give up every single member of your family and your memories, in exchange for the admiration of strangers. It is never truly worth it. I think you know that yourself deep down."

She nodded and her face changed almost imperceptibly. It held an unfathomable expression. "Yes. I suspect, I suppose, you are correct. That is fundamentally true."

We sat beside each other, in silence, for a little while longer. And it did not feel quite as unbearable as I first thought.

1 November 1861
The Rectory, Palm Cottage
Gillingham, England

Autumn was full of leaves and letters – from James, from Edward. I did not respond to either after replying to the first from each with my demurrals. I did not want to live in the fallacy of Edward's dreams, nor did I want to live in the cold practicality of James's world. I was not yet willing to rise and leave all that I called home; I was neither prepared nor excited to mould myself into someone else's passive companion. That had been my story for too long already and it was a narrative arc drafted neither by my hand nor my wishes. I did not feel I could keep doing that to myself. There was something inherently adjacent about that life, the sense that one was simply a facet of another person's story. Not that either James or Edward seemed to grasp this. Their messages, long handwritten letters, grew increasingly urgent, and continued in earnest. However benevolently they wrote, each was a declaration of *their* want. Our life together from their perspective.

I wondered what it might be like if I were asked by either of them to truly conceive of a life that I might enjoy. I debated breaking my self-imposed silence with a response carrying these thoughts, a response with a request. But then James left the country; I was surprised by how rejected that made me feel. I knew he had *work* to think about, whatever that entailed. He had businesses abroad and away he went, busying himself with what I could not imagine. Employment makes me think of the middle classes; landowners and the work that involved was the fairly visible pastime of the upper classes, but business was altogether unfamiliar. Edward continued to write, but I found I looked at his letters less. As though sensing my limited patience for verbose pages, Edward took to sending me poetry, written in short stanzas on crisp pages with flowers crushed between them. The verse was occasionally his own, but most of the time, thankfully, he borrowed his words from Keats. It was lovely of him. That much I felt. The gestures seemed ornamental though, the letters so impersonal they could be pinned to a wall, the petals enhancing an existing aesthetic. Whatever the use, it was external, for others, not for me. But I was grateful for the distraction, for the visual excitement, as James had grown silent.

I told Alice about Edward's proposal. He is lovelorn, I suggested. Lovelorn and all the rest. She was pleased for me, but guarded, her tone supportive but sober. At the time I was too consumed with thoughts in my own head to inquire as to why. I was taking long walks by myself until suddenly the Reverend began to join me.

"Sarah, have you heard from the Queen?" he asked one day as he joined me, walking straight out of the Rectory. He walked in step with me, matching my strolls, which must have been hard. I am that much shorter than him; he was having to take unusually slow steps. It would have been funny, but his joining me on a morning stroll was out of the ordinary and so I felt anxious as we went.

"I have had many letters from the Queen. She is stunned that I am not marrying. I am not ... I declined the proposals that were made."

"Proposals?" The Reverend looked at me and I stopped.

"Yes." *Darn!*

"You had more than one?"

Stop talking, Bonetta!

"James proposed multiple times," I said, hurriedly.

"Ah," he said, fixing me with a gaze that pierced my lies. "Well, the Queen is dissatisfied. And her displeasure has now reached our ears. She has asked that we intervene to advise you."

She thinks you can advise me?

The Reverend seemed to read my thoughts. "She had requested we try, and I did not think it prudent to dissuade her of that notion lest she strive for more effective tactics."

I laughed with uncertainty. And as we walked through the rustling leaves, I suspected that neither of us really wanted to talk very much about marriage. I was never one of those young women who thought and talked excitedly about her prospective husband and babies.

I liked to assume that it was my deeper intellect and all the rest. But really, I would just rather talk at length about the books that the Reverend was reading, which kept my interest far more than whatever gossip or conversation was unfolding about who was marrying whom. Now, I enjoy gowns and dresses as much as the next woman, and I really do like a ceremony and a ball. But those always struck me as moments to experience; I could never quite understand how talking about them did anything at all. I think the Reverend was the same, although I cannot be sure he would have enjoyed balls or grand occasions more broadly. Certainly, in his service to the Crown over the years, he has largely declined many such invitations. I doubt that Elizabeth knows the extent to which he has done so, and I feel bad for her, because I suspect she would quite enjoy going.

In any case, we ambled along and the Reverend said, "I have been dispatched to interrogate what your hesitations are, and get you to put them aside."

"Do you think that is going to work?"

"I think listening to people is always a good idea."

"Are you going to listen to me about my feelings, or am I to listen to you and your instructions?"

"Well, that is rather the question, is it not? I would say that it may behoove you to listen to my instructions. After which point, you can illuminate the parts that you found useful and the parts that do not serve, and articulate what your particular concerns happen to be. I will do my best to address them."

This seemed like an unnecessarily lengthy way to go about things but, again, it did not seem prudent to challenge.

"We can certainly take that route." *Circuitous, though it may be*, I said to myself, and I chuckled aloud.

He barely noticed, too busy was he taking on, with gusto, the assignment he had been given. "Well," he began, and my heart sank. "It is quite the thing to be a spouse."

I had to bite my tongue. Was this meant to be a compelling speech?

"There are many people who are more intellectual. And they may find the whole marital dance a little superfluous. I myself was one such person. And I married late. But I was fortunate that there was still one inclined towards –" he swallowed, awkwardly – "the prospect of marriage to a wiry old servant of God, who could only offer the Rectory in terms of housing and was going to have them travel the world as missionaries. Many young women, even those with a thirst for adventure, do not want to spend their childrearing years ferrying children on actual ferries."

I chuckled.

He smiled. As if buoyed on, he continued. "And there are many such people, including some women, who are too thoughtful, too smart and too curious to be interested in the marital dance. I suspect that you are one such woman. This is difficult enough, but in a country like ours it is doubly difficult for you, as you are already of African descent. To be uncommon in another additional way is not necessarily an asset."

I chuckled again, this time in disbelief.

"As such, I would think it would be in your interest to take the first proposal that happens to come your way."

I wondered how he might respond if he knew the first proposal was from Edward? Would he still be encouraging me to accept a proposal from an English nobleman?

"I would also suggest that," at this point, his voice lowered and softened from the strident rhetoric that had echoed around the field , "given you lost so much of your birth family, it may well be of value to you to have a family. Many of us can take for granted that there are people in our lives; you do not have that. You have the monarch, but she is old. Her children, they will marry off their offspring, and who can say whether the obligations that they will feel towards you will include financial ones? They most certainly shall not. And even if the Queen leaves you a small fortune, you lack experience in this sphere. Have you managed your own household before? Have you spent your own money?"

I had not. But contrary to what he thought, that idea did not scare me. In fact, it suddenly struck me as a thrilling opportunity. That was what I should do. I should actively choose not to wed, then I need not worry about the suitors that come for my hand. It would also mean I could ignore any that did. Instead, I could ask the Queen to allow me to manage my own fortune – that which she had set aside for me in the event of her death – and move into and manage a home for myself somewhere. The Queen could easily find a place for me – a house perhaps in Windsor. I would not be asking to be made a chatelaine. Something grand in aesthetic but not in size would suffice. One of the many properties that the Queen herself owns that remains primarily empty – was that something I could move into? Could I not take rooms in one such residence and live for myself? Suddenly the possibilities before me seemed endless. It started with me living for myself. Being able to make decisions…

I was smiling. The Reverend could tell that my mind had gone off in a different direction.

"So," he said, and repeated himself until I looked directly at him. "Why not tell me your objections to the whole situation?"

But I had lost interest in the topic. For now, rather than complaining about the unsatisfying prospects, I had a solution, in the form of a different proposal. First to myself and then to the Queen.

My gaze was directed inwards. "I have just realized I had a letter I needed to send…"

The Reverend raised his eyebrows, as though he could not believe what was happening.

"I am sorry, is this terribly rude of me?"

"Not at all. I am pleased that my advice has proven so useful..." He stopped speaking, as if he did not want to risk damaging what was unfolding. "You do that which makes sense." He all but chivvied me back to the Rectory. As I walked away, I could feel the strength of his smile against my back.

I wrote my letter and sent it straight to the Queen.

7 November 1861
Clifton Hill
Brighton, England

The Queen's reply was swift. If one could call it a reply. It was a letter addressed to the Schoens. I was instructed to pack my things. I was moving to Sussex. We had been sitting in the kitchen. Elizabeth had been going through the letters that had arrived. There was one that was clearly from the Court addressed to the Schoens. And not me. This never happened. I may have been under their guardianship, but correspondence from the Court came to me.

"Did you receive a letter, Sally?" she asked.

"I did not," I said, feeling bemused.

"Yes," the Reverend said at the same time, having reached into the outstanding pile and spotted what looked like a similar one addressed to me. "There was one also for Bonetta."

I reached out and took it, confused about what it could be.

Elizabeth was halfway through reading hers when she threw it down on the floor. "NO."

The Reverend looked at her. All the babes at the table, faces dirty and food all over them, stopped and looked at her as well. Sticky fingers hovered over their cheeks and on the dishes on the table. Their faces were so fat and round and full. They looked adorable. I looked back to the letter and wondered what was written that had so repelled Mrs Schoen?

I read the letter aloud:

Dear Sarah,

I have sent you this correspondence on behalf of Her Majesty, the Queen. She has kindly arranged for you to move into your new premises living with the Brumhards in Brighton, starting tomorrow. By the time you receive this letter, someone will have been dispatched to the Schoens' address in Sussex to collect all your things and take them ahead to Brighton. The Brumhards are excited to welcome you into their home. This concludes your stay with the Schoens. I hope you use this evening to thank them for their generous hospitality. It would be prudent of you to focus on your goodbyes; the Crown's courtier will handle your preparations and move to Brighton, just as the Crown has always assisted in your prior relocations.

Yours sincerely,

(An incomprehensible signature)

On behalf of Her Majesty, Queen Victoria

I kept the letter close to me, for this precise moment when I could write it down word for word. I knew I would want to ensure the letter was saved exactly as it was written. I could too easily see a future world where the Queen refused to acknowledge what she had instructed.

She had power on her side. But I would always have the truth.

Annie jumped up. "She is punishing you! She is pushing you. She is terrible. She is terrible!" *Her words were my thoughts.*

"No," the Reverend said sternly. "No, Annie, we do not say that about Her Majesty the Queen."

Annie protested. "She is ... she is ... she is very much ... you cannot make someone move. Etta is not a puppet. This is outrageous..." Her voice held a wail.

Frederick punched a wall.

"Your father is right," Elizabeth said finally.

The Schoens and I looked on in surprise at her. It was a plausible response from her. More expected than her outburst earlier. She was more acquiescent to power than most, but I did not expect her to be so willing to thrust me onto another family.

"It is important," she said, her voice calm and her hands trembling, "that we adhere to the contents of the letter."

As Elizabeth said this she was actually tearing the Schoens' letter into shreds. She did not appear to have grasped what her hands were doing. "It is a letter of instruction from the Queen. And we are to obey it because she is the Queen. We are subjects. It matters little what we might think." There was another tearing sound as she reduced it to strips. The whole thing fell into pieces. She reached for the envelope from both my letter and hers and threw them both into the nearby fire.

The Schoen children were looking momentarily reassured. The Reverend was shocked. All of them turned to look at me. I could not say anything. I realized that they were unsure how I felt; whether I was even sad about the proceedings. I was. I did not know who these people in Brighton were. I had no say in what was taking place. I was thrown; I was not expecting this. It was a betrayal. Of all the things I have talked about, all the things that I have complained about. The worst was the powerlessness – the feeling that one is controlled, that one has little autonomy over who they are and how they have to show up in this world. To be moved again is to be subject to a cross-section of my worst fears. Unpleasant surprises, a loss of control, separation from family... The Queen knew that nothing else would make me feel so alone.

I knew at that moment that I could not forgive her. That I could never love her again, that I could never trust her again. She had taken my deepest vulnerability and used it against me to prove that she would get what she wanted, or I would suffer more than I realized I had suffered already. That there was always more she could punish me with if I did not submit to her will. I did not say anything. I just stood and stared at the Schoens.

They stared back. Indignant, sad, a little hesitant, with what looked like love in their eyes. I sat back down. I held the letter to my chest. A tear rolled onto my cheek. I cried in front of them. My head bent, chin on my chest, while I sobbed. The kitchen help and the nanny ushered the children out of the kitchen, or they tried to. I heard the small children's pattering footsteps. I felt soft, sticky fingers on my skin and half-formed voices struggling to pronounce my name. They were hurried away. The room was emptied of Schoens and staff, except the four of them: the Reverend, Elizabeth, Annie and Frederick.

They stood huddled together at one end of the table and I at the other. There was silence but for my sobs. But they were holding the end of the table. And my face was pressed into my arms, folded across the tabletop at the other end. But holding on to the table, it felt like they were holding me – holding me still – for a moment. Just before I was to be set adrift, vicariously through the old rickety wood, I was being held.

Brighton was cold, chilly. The air was crisp, clear. I wondered if this would be better for my lungs, which is not the excuse that will be given, not that one was offered this time. Officially, was one even needed? Aged eighteen, as I am, there is no requirement of a ward.

28 December 1861
Clifton Hill
Brighton, England

The best that could be said about the Brumhards is that they did not like to talk too much. I had arrived after a long and uneven journey by carriage with a courtier who kept his face in a book for the duration of the trip. We stopped in front of a townhouse that gleamed a colonial white. The terraced houses formed a perfect square around a private garden; a key was required to access it.

I waited in the carriage while the courtier and the coachman struggled with boxes and cases I barely recognized. *What was even in there?* Looking back, I regret whatever impulse stopped me from asking outright. The courtier spoke quietly with the Brumhards while the coachman acted like a footman and took my things all the way into the house. The Brumhards were an elderly couple – one of those couples that have begun to morph into each other. At a glance it could be hard to tell, when seated, which Brumhard was which.

After the coachman and the courtier had left, the Brumhards and I stood unmoving in the hallway. Finally, the taller Brumhard, a hunched man with a pinched face and rheumy eyes, extended a knob-bled finger to me and gestured for me to follow him. He walked towards a cold drawing room with a high ceiling where the fireplace stood empty. "Can you make a fire?" he asked.

I was incredulous. Was I a scullery maid? Why on Earth was he asking me this?

"Her Majesty, the Queen of England, had never requested that I learn, so no, I am afraid I cannot. Whoever usually tends to your fireplace shall have to continue."

"Well, we do things a little differently to the Queen of England. You will have to get used to that."

"Yes, it appears I shall," I said, in as arch a tone as I could muster.

At this point his wife shuffled into the room. She pushed past me with almost comical slowness and took a deep and pointed sniff. Why did they even agree to take me in, I wondered, if it was such an affront to have me here?

"But since you are so fond of titles, you can call me 'Mr Brumhard' and my wife 'Mrs Brumhard'." Mr Brumhard offered something of a wolfish smile.

A less charitable reading might say he bared his teeth at me.

"We have..." Mrs Brumhard spoke from behind me and trailed off as I turned around to face her.

"We have rules in this house. We are old, as you can see, and we do not have a castle of courtiers to help us each day. The pantry is locked.

Thomas, our ... the young fellow who lives here, he's a Brumhard and he knows the pantry is kept locked. It is not a punishment, mind. We are just careful." Mr Brumhard added the last part hastily, perhaps fearful of what correspondence I might send to the court. I almost snickered. Surely it was clear if I had been banished here, that nobody cared whether I ate or not?

"You will eat when the clock strikes six. Your dinner will be prepared and left for you in the dining room. We do not do breakfast here. I trust that will suit you fine. Young ... *girls* –" here Mrs Brumhard faltered – "even young girls such as yourself prefer a slim figure and a modest diet. I am certain that this will suffice."

I nodded.

Mrs Brumhard turned to her husband. "Would you like to show her to her room?"

He shook his head. "I can get up those stairs once a day, and I save that for night-time."

"This house has five bedrooms and only one is empty."

I must have frowned because Mrs Brumhard interjected. "Only one of the bedrooms has your belongings in it. All the others have our personal items. Since you have enjoyed the comforts of a castle, I am certain you can find your way to the bedroom with little trouble."

"Yes, Mrs Brumhard."

She made a slow shooing motion with her hand. I looked at it and back at her. She looked at me defiantly, as if to say, *Yes?*

"How will I receive my allowance?"

"I beg your pardon?"

"The Queen will have made provisions for my expenses and any needs I might have."

As if in unison, their eyes hardened. "It is with those provisions that we can provide you with food and board."

This was a nightmare. *They* were a nightmare.

"I was referring to additional costs. Train fare, for example."

Mr Brumhard did not speak for a moment. His mouth flattened into a line and he looked at his wife.

"When they wish for you to return they will send a carriage," she said, her tone matter-of-fact.

"And if I wish to take a train?"

"We have the garden," Mr Brumhard interrupted quickly, relief filling his face.

"Will I be granted a key to the garden?"

"Your own key?" Mrs Brumhard was incredulous. "Are these the trifles you would expect us to spend money on for you? Having an additional key cut for your fleeting visit?"

"I apologize, Mrs Brumhard," I said, not bothering to sound sincere. She was tiresome and I made sure she knew it. "Would I be able to use the key you already have, from time to time, or would this be too much trouble?"

"Trouble? It would not be 'trouble'!" Mr Brumhard insisted. "Who said—"

"It would be a reward, though," Mrs Brumhard intervened, sleekly. "I will personally provide you with the key from time to time as a reward for good behaviour."

"Nature is not a treat. It should be for everyone."

"For everyone? Not everyone has access to the same opportunities. I do not make the rules. There are barriers and structures and hierarchies and orders everywhere. You may be a 'princess' in Africa and a 'protégée' in Queen Victoria's court—"

"In Queen Victoria's *country*," I said, but I was starting to think that I needed a key for my bedroom.

"Well, you are a ... an orphan here. In different places, in different countries, you may receive different treatment. Here in Brighton, in my house, when we take you in as our charitable duty to ... *Her Majesty* the Queen, you abide by our rules. And the rules state that people like you do not have access to the private garden as an automatic rule."

"People like me?"

The words hung in the air. Mrs Brumhard looked defiant but did not say anything. In the end it was Mr Brumhard who punctured the strained hostility.

"Tenants, visitors, guests. The private gardens are for the people who own the houses on the square. We pay a yearly fee to have the gardens maintained. Access is not guaranteed for visitors. It is subject to the rules of the host. And for Mrs Brumhard, it requires your good behaviour."

I nodded mutely.

"Now, will you please go upstairs to your room?"

He did not add *and stay there*, but it was clear that venturing downstairs for anything besides dinner would constitute poor behaviour by comparison. I did not know what I should or could have done differently. I would replay that conversation in my mind. Should I have asked about my financial independence instead of expenses? What else could I have said?

The room I was assigned did not have a window and the hard, old bed filled all the available space. There was almost nothing else in the room, as there was nowhere for anything else to go. The coachman had been directed to put the cases in a far larger room with full-length windows and a Juliet balcony that overlooked the private gardens. I had retired to this room first. But Mrs Brumhard had come to tell me there would be no dinner that night as I had probably eaten my meal on the journey down. Catching me in that room, she screeched at me until I fled from it and continued shouting until I was in the windowless one across the hall. I think they set that up deliberately. I want to say they are cruel, but the word itself is too kind.

The cases could not fit in the room with me, and I had to open them out onto the corridor. It contained my belongings, but my belongings from my childhood: a large number of dresses I had not worn for at least five years. I could not wear the clothes with which I had been sent to Brighton. There was no money for new ones, no money for travelling out here and no escape into nature – no possible peace of mind.

How could she do this to me?

HOW COULD SHE DO THIS TO ME?

I was imprisoned. She had banished me to Brighton, abandoned me with these people, punished me with her silence. I was in hell.

1 January 1862
Clifton Hill
Brighton, England

One month after I had moved in, I received a letter from the Queen. As I recognized the handwriting on the envelope, a curl of rage leapt at my throat. The ink on the outside was blotched. I wondered if it had been raining in London. Every day seemed a rainy one in Brighton. Of course, I could only refer to the days I had actually left my room and seen the world outside. I knew the letter would disappoint me. Her perennially good cheer when another might be in pain would no doubt be in full force today.

The letter was damp. I would not be surprised if the Brumhards had tried to steam it open and thus wet it that way, not that they seemed curious about me or the Queen. Their enthusiasm I spied only once, and realized it was in receipt of their payment for housing me. With the pages so damp, I braced myself for a letter with more painting than prose. I felt a sigh of frustration. I scanned the letter for the meat of it; I was uninterested in pleasantries. A line jumped out at me.

Sally, he is dead. My husband is dead.

My heart. It tightened a little, my throat felt constricted.

I have lost the last person who could call me by my name.

I kept reading. The ink was splodged on the word Sally, like a tear had landed and made that word its home.

It was not until March of 1862 that I was invited back to Windsor. And I did not try to come sooner than that. I am no good with funerals, with the deaths of others. It did not seem prudent to offer anything I did not have. I did not have love to give. I could, from afar, muster a level of empathy. But were I to be before them all in the opulent beauty of the castles and the proximity of their loved ones, and remember where I was returning to: barren land, a home divested of warmth, comfort, aesthetics, or anything even remotely familiar ... well, my anger might show too clearly on my face when I was meant to be joining them in grieving. I had privately mourned Prince Albert. I had been fond of him and he of me. I felt guilty for not having seen him at all in the last two years of his life. I had let my frustrations with the Queen eclipse my relationship with him as an individual. It had been a mistake. He had something of the Reverend about him. They were both scientists in the purest sense of the word. They were investigators, knowledge seekers. I always felt safest with such people. They wanted to study; they wanted to learn. They were blunt and awkward and they cared not for formalities nor frivolities. I felt safe among such people. They knew what truly mattered.

He had been good for the Queen; she had needed someone to channel her frustrations and express her desires. She had chafed against the particular strictures of palace life. She was always in need of an outlet. But there were useful ways in which to do so. Banishing me to Brighton was not one of them. Had Prince Albert been well, I doubt she could have got away with making that decision. I felt certain he would have questioned the choice.

When I arrived, rather than going first to Windsor, I went to St James's Palace. It was quite a delight to see Princess Alice. But while I arrived with my usual optimism, she was still grieving. I expected this, of course, but somehow it took me by surprise. She was present and yet it was as though part of her, too, had departed.

"Have you spoken to Edward? I sent him word of my arrival; I have not heard much in the way of response." I thought it might be nice to reconvene; his letters had kept me company during those long and lonely Brighton months. It had been a winter irrespective of the weather outside. It had been a prison for the mind as much as the body. And thus, while I had felt impatience towards his flimsy words when I had a relatively comfortable life, in the absence of hope and freedom, feeling subsumed in human frailty, his fanciful language was a light, the dreaminess there had a place. Without a life of my own to look forward to, his letters were the world I would escape into.

So bleak was life with the Brumhards in Brighton that I would take his letters, filled with proposals and puppies, wild worlds and sailing fantasies, and I would cradle them to my chest each night. I would sleep with the words seeping into my brain, envisioning myself roaming free. It was exactly what I needed. I did not tell Alice this. I did not even ask her whether her mother planned on liberating me from that hovel she had banished me to. Or whether she might have pleaded my case with her. I repeated my comments about Edward, with perhaps a touch of urgency in my voice.

Coolly, Alice asked, "Well, I wonder if he has told his betrothed you have arrived."

I stared aghast. "He is ... he is ... to be wed? How is he to be wed? He has still been sending me letters!"

"He would not be the first betrothed person to send letters to another love, now, would he?" Alice looked at me pointedly. Her eyes were bereft of their sparkle. In their absence, I felt I was being chided.

I was silent. The silence stretched.

Alice broke it first. "My wedding will be in July. I should hope they let you out to attend. You are ultimately as rebellious as I; if you wanted to go somewhere you could. Which is why it surprised me that I had not seen you all this time..."

"How could I have gone anywhere? The Brumhards did not give me any money. Unlike the Schoens, who—"

"It was Mama," Alice cut in.

"Yes. Yes. But that money was given to the Schoens, who chose to grant it to me as an allowance. This family does not let me have train fare."

Alice frowned but did not speak.

"So how can I ... how can I be bold? Who can I call for a brougham? It is hard enough to get my letters sent out! Who is going to stand up for me when the Queen is rejecting me – *banishing me*, flinging me from her as though I were some thief in the night?" My voice had risen. Alice looked outside, at the garden under her window. I was annoyed, but I was surprised that I had forgotten how to mask that. I spent so much time in Brighton consumed with rage, it did not occur to me that I should instinctively know better.

Again Alice said nothing.

I wished she could understand what I had been through. It was clear that she could not.

"Edward," I began defensively, "has sent me letters telling me to think of nothing but what we will do when we are to be united once more. Insisting it is only a matter of time. What is that meant to mean? If it does not involve us being wed, then, lest we forget, he has already proposed to me before. With the explicit words, *marry me*."

Tonelessly, she said "How long ago was that?"

"A year."

"And what was your response?"

"I declined."

"And after that, he continued to write and you continued to write back."

"Yes."

"Did you talk again about marriage?"

"N-not explicitly. No."

"So then perhaps he assumed you no longer wanted to marry him?"

"Well, I ... I did not know. I did not realize I was supposed to expect that he would go and marry someone else soon after. That his feelings for me were that fleeting – that I was such a fleeting moment in another's life."

Alice just looked at me. "It appears that there was more to the story."

"More...? How?"

"His mother may have been aware that his attentions were venturing towards the aristocrat who was also a princess, the ward of the Queen. This was unacceptable to her."

"Oh." Another day, another rejection.

"She orchestrated the introduction between Edward and the woman to whom he is now betrothed."

So he is weak. I knew it in my heart. *He is weak as I, full of dreams. Never willing to try.*

Late in the day I was taken to Windsor Castle. Fog hovered in the sky. The castle, usually so windy that walking into any room at the height of summer will still grant the visitor a terrible chill, was humid. The air was tight and trapped. I wondered when the Queen had last allowed the windows to be opened. Was she trying to ensure that no air left the rooms of the castle lest they take the essence of Prince Albert with them?

When I finally saw the Queen she was clad completely in black. She wore a veil indoors. She spoke little. I sat opposite her in silence for what felt like hours. Eventually, she asked me, dully, her eyes barely lifting from the black velvet of her gloves.

"Will you marry James Pinson Labulo Davies?"

The question hung between us in the vacant space where Prince Albert's energy once lived.

2 April 1862
St James's Palace
London, England

"Well, hello."

I turned up at the door of the Schoens' unannounced. Yes, as somebody who loathes surprises, this is more than a touch hypocritical of me. I grant you that. But they have never said they hate surprises. It was me that proved so prickly and difficult about such things.

The front door opened and the Reverend gazed out at me for a moment. Then, almost impulsively, he took me by the arm and led me to the kitchen. I overtook him and marched forward, pushing open the door. The Schoens were gathered; they saw me, they rose, they were speechless, tearful, stunned and overwhelmed. Am I back? How long am I back for, am I staying with them? Did the Queen decide this? They had not heard anything.

As the questions whirled around the room, I silently went over and gave Elizabeth a hug. She looked at me. I rather wished she would say, *I told you so*. I wanted to say, *You were right all along!*

But what was she right about? She never told me to be grateful that she was taking me in. But I did not know how bad it could be.

"I have missed you," I said, and waited for her face to morph into a kind of pious self-satisfaction.

But she just said, "So did we!" and pulled me into an even tighter hug. And I regretted having instigated the first, as it was now impossible to get out of the next. Goodness, would she ever let me go? I actually had a purpose for the visit. I was not simply there to surprise them.

The Reverend and his wife were interrupted by a troop of slightly older-looking, grumpy-faced babes, who rose from the table and could now run and say my name with actual words as opposed to just half-coherent songs that began, "Sour Sally, sour Sally." It was strange to hear the young children sing my name as Sally, even though they had made up the song before I left. Of course, Elizabeth had been calling me Sally to her children in my absence. And, dear me, was it not *bright* in here? The sun streamed in and the air was so fresh. The smell of cooking, the sound of playful laughter, was like a salve to my soul, brightening the day.

"What is Brighton like?" Frederick asked. His voice was the same, but he had grown another five inches since I had seen him last. He was handsome all of a sudden, and broad-shouldered. I could not recall exactly how old he was. But he looked older than I.

How was Brighton? My face fell before I could say anything.

Following close behind him was Annie. But she looked wary. "What does this mean?"

I tried to put on a smile. But something in her expression killed it before it reached halfway across my face.

"You are not returning to Brighton?"

I shook my head.

"So you are to be married off, then?"

I faltered.

"So the Queen won. Her little power play?"

I wanted to remind Annie that Prince Albert had died, but I shrivelled in the face of her disdain.

"Annie, I have a special treat for you!" Why did I need to say that so loudly to everyone? There was no reason to make it a performance, but I think I felt bad at not having contacted her – none of it having been deliberate. And thus I felt like we needed a bit of ceremony. This is, of course, the purpose of a monarchy in the first place. We ought to be collectively excited about something. I brandished a very elegant-looking envelope at her.

"I come today with an invitation."

"OK…"

"And with…" At this, I slipped back to the brougham, and returned with…

"A gown?!"

Annie stared at me.

"The gown is for the event this evening. Thus, if some adjustments might need to be made, as I had to guess your measurements, there is more than enough time; we shall do it at the palace. Tonight there is a garden party being thrown by my dear friend Princess Alice ahead of her upcoming wedding. And Annie, are my guest."

Elizabeth stared at me. She clapped and squeaked. Everyone was up in arms. And I was thrilled because *this* was what I was here for. This was the hope. It was also a nice deflection: there were no questions about what this meant. Was I still living in Brighton? What was next?

I said, "Since time is of the essence, I apologize that this is just a fleeting visit," knowing full well that Elizabeth would be so thrilled that I was elevating her beloved daughter that she would not care if I never saw her again. "But I do have to take Annie with me to St James's Palace right now, because if the dress needs some fitting or changing, we will need to retain the seamstresses while they're still here. Soon they shall leave to assist with the rest of the royal attendees to the garden party and so forth."

"Of course," said Elizabeth Schoen.

The Reverend looked between her and Annie. He was shocked, but nodded. "Well, it is always a delight to see you. I hope this means we will see you again more often."

Elizabeth looked at him as if realizing something. Her face started to change, taking on the questions his comments had inadvertently evoked. *What does this mean? What has Sarah agreed to?* Before we could have further conversation, I gestured for Annie to "Come, come." We quickly left the Rectory and jumped into the waiting brougham to be driven very smartly away.

Annie was so excited, she just wanted to talk. She did not want to be asked questions. So, I opened the box and held it aloft in the carriage and we squealed over every single bit of the design. When I told her this was her gown to keep, not something to borrow, she almost fell from the carriage with excitement. And I was happy; a positive thing had been achieved. And when I brought her to St James's Palace, to the apartment where I had been staying with Alice, her eyes grew round like saucers and she gazed about her, saying, "My goodness." Standing in a dressing room, she asked, "You sleep here?"

"I do not."

It did not seem a prudent moment to admit that nobody sleeps there.

"Look, let us be quick. I need to see how it fits." I made her try it on. I made her walk and strut and stroll. The dress fit perfectly. And then, before she would ask me more questions, I had her help me choose between two gowns for myself. As I tried each one I invited her to think about adjustments she may want. Or that my gown might need. Did we want feathers, amendments to the bust, silk ribbons added to the waist? I insisted on having the seamstresses join us. They looked irritated at first, but they did like me. They were discreet – and they loved Annie. I think they loved the joy in her surprise. They also found her beautiful: she was blonde and bright-eyed. As I said once before, she was not the only one of the Schoen children to take the looks that had once been bestowed on Elizabeth, to carry off the shine born to her. Although, to be honest, perhaps after quite so many months in the dreariness of Brighton and among the endless grey men hovering around the palaces and castles, Elizabeth looked as radiant as a star. Annie, blonde and glowing, looked little different. Perhaps there was something in the human experience of working life, of actual people among people, that gave beauty and vividness to the skin and cheeks. I thought back to the castle, to the airless swarms of aristocrats isolated and buttoned up, and the Queen mute and resolute, her veil like a self-imposed muzzle. She might have been grieving, but that whole sphere was a stultified and sad. I was mentally brought back to Brighton with a shudder. Annie, catching my expression in the mirror, turned from it to ask me a question.

"We shall be late!" I insisted, taking Annie's hand. I hurried her outside. The garden party was exquisite. In all the time I had been to these – and I had been to many of the garden parties over the years – I had never really taken stock of all the little things that made that perfect summer party precisely what it was. Perhaps I had more reason to be interested in *keeping a home* than I once was. Or perhaps the Brighton banishment meant everything was bathed in the elevated glow of the unfamiliar. Or maybe there really was something extraordinary about these garden ornaments. The glass statues and carefully placed chairs, the floating stones that were set as a little pathway across the waters. It was all so beautiful, so delicate and carefully rendered. I wondered to myself whether I would oversee something like this or whether Alice herself oversaw this, and this might be how she would decorate a garden with her husband for their own parties. I formally introduced Alice to Annie – I could not recall if they had met. Annie was rather awed but Alice was so nonchalant and cheeky that they quickly fell into easy conversation.

"I say," Annie said. "There's only one African man here. I am going to assume ... is that James? There cannot be that many ... such men that the Queen knows so well to be brought ... invited here. Are there?" She was slightly tripping over her words; she clearly did not wish to offend. We had come a long way, I remembered, from the 'collar' remark. I found myself remembering and winced. And then I thought hard about what she said. James was *here*. I turned to Alice.

"James is here?"

"Why is that a surprise? Why would your betrothed not be here?"

If I had wanted him here, he would have been my guest. But he is not, that is why Annie is here. Alice, who is more sister than friend,

216

immediately understood my thoughts.

"I apologize. I assumed because you had accepted him that—"

"You accepted him?" Annie froze. It was unclear whether Annie was furious with me because I had not told her, or stunned that I was getting married. And I could not tell even how I felt about this. Had I sunk in her estimation, by getting married? Did I want to sink in her estimation? Suddenly I was back to having a number of people's opinions to think about and be validated by. I wanted to let that approach to life go. I wanted to let this roll off me, like morning dew that has landed on one's sleeve. But I did care about her opinion. And I did not want her to feel deceived. She was already out of her depth in a place like this. And she looked somewhat hurt.

"Well, let me introduce you to him," I said. "You two have never met." I paused. I was not sure why I was quite so keen on this plan. I needed to distract her from feeling bereft but also give her what she wanted, which was some sort of access or introduction or insight. My skin felt cold despite the evening warmth. I remembered her calling him a brute a year ago. Would she insult him again? I braced myself. He came over to me...

"Sarah, you look enchanting." He smiled.

"This is Annie," I said as flatly as I could manage. "Annie is the daughter of the Schoens. And she is my guest here today."

Annie stepped forward. She held out her hand to James. A show of goodness. I just felt awkward. I turned to leave. And then to my complete horror, I spotted Edward. What on earth was Alice thinking? Why had she invited him? He was by himself, lingering by a table laden with food. I looked around briefly and then hurried off to speak to him. He looked at me. His face went bright red. The crimson stretched right up his neck, into his cheeks and into his hair, which was darker than it was a year ago. It also seemed thinner. His eyes, however, were as gentle and ardent as ever. They seemed a little hollow. He seemed a little hollow.

"Edward," I said when I was right in front of him.

"Sarah." He dipped into a low bow. "Sarah. You look beautiful. More illuminating than the grounds themselves! I daresay the garden must be jealous. I know I would be."

"How are you?"

"I am terribly well, how are you?"

"I am in the mood to congratulate. Congratulations, Edward. I hear you are betrothed!"

He reddened lightly once more. "I hear you are as well."

"Well, I think I had less choice."

"I think you made your choice."

"As did you. My choice was made *for* me. You are a man with an estate. You are set to inherit. You have far more autonomy that you realize."

"Life is less simple than you may want to accept," he said gently, but I felt patronized and annoyed. How little he knew of the more difficult lives a person could lead. It felt ridiculous to have found him worth talking to, in all his tortured naivety. I did not offer a reply. I walked away, disappointed in him and myself.

14 September 1862
Somewhere on the seas
Exact location unknown

We spent the night before the wedding in a little rented cottage that the Queen had gifted to us…

It is strange to write about myself with a collective noun, 'we'. 'We' refers to the girls who were to be my bridesmaids and I, not to James and I, and while it feels like a natural way to reflect on what followed, even a month later, I bristle as I write these words. Am I already betraying myself by subsuming my identity into my married state, or my presence in the 'wedding party' ahead of the main event? Women do this all the time. So much is made of brides and their weddings one could hardly consider this a surprise. Perhaps because it seemed so clear that I would not make one of these matches written about in society magazines, I had considered myself apart from that narrative. There were no African weddings in *The Lady*, after all.

Or perhaps it was less nefarious than that. After all, Queen

Victoria was never subsumed by her marriage. She adored her prince but she was still very much her own person. I do not think I am close to feeling anything for James that could rival the great love story of 'Victoria and Albert'. But I wonder how long such love can take to build.

It is not the question on my mind today – or tonight, rather. And given how rare it has been to catch a quiet night undisturbed by the raucousness of seamen or invitations to converse or the rocking motions of the water, I may as well get right to the point.

Which is to state that for better or worse, imaginary reader, in the words of Charlotte Brontë, *I married him*.

We were wed in the Church of St Nicholas in Brighton, not altogether far from the house in Clifton Hill to which I was banished until I agreed to it. From the outside the whole area is quite beautiful, with straight, square houses gleaming a stucco white. It is astonishing what loneliness and strangers can do even to settings as beautiful as they. Imprisonment is primarily a state of mind. Or maybe every mood is.

The days leading up to the wedding are a blur now, but I think they were a blur then, too. Who organized everything? Elizabeth and Annie, assisted by courtiers of the Queen? Was James presiding over such matters? It was certainly not me. I remember how, when the carriages arrived at the cottage in which I spent my final night as an unmarried woman, I barely knew the address of the venue and whether the Queen owned it and simply donated it for the night or whether it was leased for the occasion.

"I thought we would be in Windsor," I muttered to Annie, who had come along. She was one of the bridal party: the women who agreed to be my bridesmaids.

"How much more beautiful is Brighton in the summer?" she whispered back, cradling my hand in the large carriage, as the other women talked loudly around us. I did not even know half the women in the bridal party and tonight I was to be joined by four others, aside from Annie. All four were West African, two were James' sisters. In different circumstances I would have been overcome with excitement, nervousness, joy. The two sharing our carriage were beautiful, so unlike everything I had been made to expect of Africans. I, the 'poised' rarity, was here among other poised African women, who wore ensembles that looked familiar enough, though the words to describe them were not. The *gele*, the *wrapper*, the *pelete bite*? I could not even place on whom I had seen these designs. It belonged to some hidden part of my life, the forgotten history, before Dahomey. In any case, all the women who had gamely agreed to be my bridesmaids joined us the night before the wedding.

I should have been curious about them, but I could barely utter a word. It was for this reason that I was so grateful Annie was present. She had seen me at my worst, and was deft enough to cover for me, to start conversations whenever they were directed at me and I inevitably stalled.

"I have never tried alcohol before!" Annie said at one point, as we piled into the cottage. The other ladies clearly had, and indulgent smiles unfolded on their faces. I watched as the coachmen carried our belongings ahead of us into the cottage.

One of James' sisters barely waited for the final coachmen to leave before marching into the centre of the sitting room and holding a bottle aloft.

I felt myself recoil.

She was not looking at me. "Well, *Annie*," she called out, a dare in her voice. "I think you are being summoned..." She turned to the other women. "It is summoning her, is it not?"

"I hear a summons!" a taller African woman, whose name I was never told, joined in.

Annie blushed and to my complete surprise began to dance her way over to the women. It was dancing I had not seen before; it did not resemble the kind I had seen at or studied ahead of court balls. The other women laughed at her movements, but not unkindly. They clapped and clapped. As she stood before them, breathless and flushed, they rewarded her with the contents of the bottle. At some point she put the wine glass to one side and drank from the mouth.

This was met with squeals of giddy laughter. At the time, I was unclear as to why. Upon reflection, I do not find the implied vulgarity funny either way.

"When is your wedding night?" someone asked her.

"Do not jest, she *is* in fact betrothed!"

"Of course she is. A bottle of wine and the clergyman's daughter disappears!" Well, she was soon to be a clergyman's wife. I was unsure what the difference would be. But Elizabeth had introduced her to every vicar's firstborn in and around Kent. In the end she had found her match with a widower who did in fact have a son, but the elder was the better match. Was she happy about her upcoming marriage? Was it a love match? In truth, I could not say. It was a financially impressive one. But as to anything else, my attentiveness had sapped during that time. It is somewhat embarrassing to realize, upon reflection.

I sat by the fireplace watching as they sang songs, rocked their hips, planted their feet and wriggled their waists to the rhythms of their music. But they consumed so many bottles that their movements soon grew sluggish, their voices began shouting words as opposed to singing them. Annie was the most inebriated of the group. I am grateful to have forgotten most of her antics that night, but they did not entice me to join in.

It did look very fun. It was full of laughter. The air was filled with their excitement. In the end I went to bed early.

"I have to show up looking fresh and alert for my wedding day," I patiently explained as I made my way to one of the bedrooms. "Nobody wants a bride who looks tired or grey."

"You cannot go grey!" Annie roared after one too many bottles of something.

"And I shan't." I smiled. She looked mollified. I kept smiling as I backed out of the room. I did not want to be pulled back in.

The women stayed awake long after I went to sleep. They did not attempt to keep quiet or be mindful that I might need my rest. I suspect inebriation makes one selfish. I was not in the mood for attention anyway. I lay down before midnight, alone in my room. Some of the women were married but, while I needed guidance, I could not ask them to advise me about my wedding to their own brother or friend. I had a flat feeling in my stomach, inevitability mingled with anxiety. I was not sure how to think conclusively about this. There was a gown, a ceremony, vows and then the rest of our lives. It seemed so swift, and discussions about the actual life together so slight, for a commitment so large.

The wedding day itself went so quickly I felt I had no time to catch my breath. Ten carriages arrived the following morning and with the coachmen came a handful of dressmakers and lady's maids to help everyone into their gowns. I stood alone with the maid as she checked for alterations, smoothing the lace of the dress and pressing closed the final buttons that led like a cobbled path from my waist to the nape of my neck. "Beautiful, Miss," she whispered, a reminder that the only people gathered that day were strangers or servants.

What lingers a month later is how unprepared I was for the fact that none of the monarchy came. The absences of the Queen and Princess Alice were expected. Dear Alice and her husband no longer even live in England. The Queen was widowed less than a year prior; I understand that her attendance so soon would be an unreasonable demand. But then I am left with the question Alice herself had. Why send us away with such haste? Why not wait until you can enjoy the event? Another two years would not have made me an 'old maid'... but such musings are useless.

Nonetheless, their absence was galling. To not have any of them represented at the church was humiliating, especially because the wedding was written about in *The Lady* after all, and naturally the absence of the monarchy was noted. 'A multicultural affair' was apparently the summary. I did not read it myself; I did not read any of the society titles that referred to it. I did not want to read what they said about the groom. On the day I refused to think about it; I did not wish to add to the anxieties.

I will not be ungracious. The Queen ensured the wedding was lavish and ornate. A procession of carriages clicked and rolled along Brighton's finest streets, and our bridal party was presented at the Church of St Nicholas like it was a royal occasion, albeit a small one.

The pews were filled and crowds of local people gathered outside. There were, among the people staring, small children with flowers. I stared through the carriage windows willing myself not to shed a tear. When I entered the church, I had a bridesmaid confirm that James' guests were seated well. There were twenty African guests seated in the front pews. I breathed a sigh. My guests were well-seated too! The monarchy may have failed to show up for me on my wedding day, but the Forbes clan did not disappoint. Not only did many of them attend, but Commander Frederick Forbes' brother, Captain George Forbes, walked me down the aisle. We had never met before. He came all the way from Scotland.

I repeat these things to myself because at the time I would often find that while I was present somewhere, anywhere, I felt far away. An event could take place with me at the centre but feel as remote as if I were watching it unfold in front of me, or retrieving a long-forgotten dream. It remains hard to articulate even now. I often cannot feel anything; it began in earnest when I was moved to Brighton and made to live there, the first time. During the wedding, that absence of feeling took centre stage and, as I have made mention of before, I can sometimes lose time. After George Forbes walked with me, my memory of the day, of the details, falters. It was a bright day, with a ceremony to match, and the pews were filled with colour. The wedding breakfast that followed was louder than I expected, longer too, and people appeared entertained. I had invited Edward.

I could not remember actually doing so, but there was an invitation with his name upon it and he did arrive in the end. I did not see him at the service. But they were at the breakfast after; he was accompanied by his betrothed. She was tall with sun-kissed hair. A willowy blonde, nothing at all like me. It was ... interesting to see the kind of woman he finds beautiful.

I dared not speak to Reverend Schoen. He had wanted to officiate the wedding. I think I may have complicated matters, for somewhere along the line Elizabeth suggested we have it in the Rectory, which would have been absurd. In declining I am certain I made some unspecific promise to involve them somehow, but the Bishop of Sierra Leone had promised to preside over the ceremony, as a personal favour to the Queen. For James, who first saw me in the orphanage there, this carried special significance. As with most of the organizing, my efforts matched my interest, which is to say I made no effort to encourage or obstruct this and I cared not at all. But I was aware that the Reverend spent much of the day with a taut smile on his face, to the extent that I saw it. He and the family left early.

My lasting memory of the whole affair is neither the dress, long and white opal like the Queen's, nor the jewels, which were Her Majesty's, sapphires that cut into the skin of my neck. Most of all, I remember my aching feet. I remember standing still for a long time, a cacophony of voices around me. Strangers talking, laughing, smiling; children dancing. It was a long day. My feet hurt. The focus was supposed to be on me. Was this how it felt to be special? Or what marriage for aristocrats was to look like? A life of being attended to without any real attention or even autonomy over oneself? I spent barely any time with James; we exchanged vows, and that was the first of our two conversations.

There was the moment when the rain began to fall and those dancing in the gardens at Westhill Lodge hurried back into the hall. The sky grew grey, crowds forming like thick brows knitted together. James, an identical frown forming on his forehead, turned to me and said, "Bonetta, I really want us to get back to the Continent as soon as possible. Once this is done."

I had not even realized he was beside me. He had not thought to say anything until then. My heart sank like a stone. I could understand, of course. I do not miss England's clammy weather, and he did not enjoy the brittle people. But he also knew how I felt about the journey ahead. Why restate this on our wedding day?

I was not enthused about the trip ahead because I was not enthused about anything. Was the home we were to make abroad going to be definitively mine? I wanted something of my own. I wanted to be able to close the door on the world. I wanted to decorate a room, a building, a garden that could never be taken away from me. Right then I felt adrift in the world. Getting married in that city, in Brighton, made me feel like a marionette doll, reminding me of my strings. Had the Queen not plucked me from Kent and thrust me upon Brighton because I asserted myself? She herself hated Brighton; she had sold the royal residence she kept there because she could not walk around in private when she stayed! Was it poetry or coincidence that meant that when I showed defiance she placed me in the one city where she had always felt powerless herself? As if displacing me was not a fundamental violation of self already. And yes, while I cannot say that on my wedding day I was filled with thoughts of my forced resettlement in Brighton, a month after the wedding it is clear that I am still chafing about it. It is unfortunate because that resentment still sits between James and me. Might I have come to wed him eventually? Perhaps. But the wedding took place because the Queen manipulated me into conceding. I do empathize with her loss of Prince Albert but ... it was difficult.

"Tell me if this is a wild idea." Annie proved the highlight of my wedding experience, when I look back upon it. I could always count on her popping up with convivial energy to spare!

"Well, go forth. What do you have in mind?"

"I may have heard your ... *husband* expressing a certain eagerness to return to what he called 'the Continent'," she began, in a tone that told me she had been inebriated for some time.

"You might have heard this, yes." I remember feeling wary all of a sudden.

"Well, would the newly married Davies enjoy some company on their trip?"

"To Africa?" I took her by the hand and marched her outside into the rain where nobody could follow us. "Are you quite serious?"

It was pouring down, flattening her hair and sopping into my eyes. Her eyes widened. "Ye-es. You think it wild?"

"I think it marvellous!" I almost shouted.

"Truly?"

"Yes!" Gaily, I cried, and grabbed her hands in a merry-go-round. "This is the best thing that has happened all day!"

She stopped dancing. We looked at each other. I was blinking rain out of my eyes and watching it fall and clump in my lower lashes. The silk of my gown was sticky and cool.

"Oh, Bonetta."

I shook my head, touched the jewels in my ears and against my neck. "I am a princess."

"Married to a rich and handsome man."

"With whom I shall travel the world."

"A venture on which I will join."

We began dancing again in our giddy circles, the rain and sweat keeping us soaked in our gowns, the wet mud of the grass sticking to our shoes. Messy, dirty and sodden and with nobody around, it was easily the most fun I had that entire day.

It was not to last.

231

The day was coming to a natural end as more people came to say their goodbyes. Annie, who had been dancing with her new friends, my other bridesmaids, all afternoon, looked like a deflated version of her earlier self as she walked over to where James and I sat, on the terrace watching the sun slowly set. Was this what drinking too much did, I remember wondering at the time. Or was she just as tired as I, ready to be taken home and put to bed with a steaming pot of tea. We may have been wives or on the brink of such, but we were girls really. We were still young girls.

"How are you returning?" I asked, and she nodded towards a carriage in the distance. "There is a carriage for you?" My eyes widened with excitement. "Your betrothed is very attentive! Why did he not come?" I had invited him after all.

Annie sighed. "He is waiting in the carriage with Father."

"How did that come about? I thought the Reverend had left."

"No, a coachman kindly took him and the others to the station earlier today, where they caught a train. Mr Wainwright told Father he would send a carriage for us, but Father was not sure it would be large enough and wanted to spare any embarrassment, I suspect."

"Well, we have a surplus of carriages today and they shan't all be in use. James and I are staying in Brighton; any carriage we take could have been returned to the church to escort you all home. Had you but said!"

"It occurred to me not."

"To me, either." The air sagged between us. Sprightly, I said, "Will you introduce me to your Mr Wainwright?"

"I think you would rather not be introduced."

Ah. I saw James look over at her. I wondered if he had come to the same conclusion as I. "Not fond of Africans is he, this shepherd of God?" I tried not to keep the mockery from my tone, but it was, by this point, humorous in a way. Was this clergyman going to declare James and I inferior after our wedding that was sponsored by the Queen, officiated by the bishop of a nation, feted with flowers by a procession of street children and attended by the editors of society's most elite titles? And if he was not a snob then on what grounds could a Christian servant as such maintain an open display of bigotry?

Annie did not answer, but she looked forlorn.

"How will he handle your sojourn to Africa next year? I had assumed he would come with."

"As had I."

I frowned. "But he shan't."

She shook her head.

I felt the slow creep of dread. "And you shan't..."

"Regretfully."

I stared as she broke eye contact, breaking my heart at the same time. I watched her retreating back in silence as she headed to where her betrothed stood, in front of a carriage he had kept waiting, so far away I could not see his face. When James finally spoke, I did not expect the words that followed. A month on and the precision eludes me, but it was some nonsense affirming her as an obedient wife.

"She is not his wife, yet."

"Exactly," he said.

I turned to him. "That is all you gathered from our exchange? She is yielding her dreams before marriage and you valorise it? And this is, then, what you expect of me? Is this the home you promised me, the princess? Is this the life I should expect? You would have me as someone to be obedient to whatever you decide, all the time?"

"I'm just pointing out the distinction, when it is royalty, aristocracy, you are happy to obey—"

"I do not wish to obey anybody," I said, my mouth tightened. "I wish to have the power to decide what I want for myself."

"You cannot have the power to decide in a country that will never see you as a woman or an aristocrat, because you are not white."

Yet Annie who is white and a woman born in this country does not have any say in her own affairs.

I did not say this. Who seeks a quarrel on their wedding day?

My husband, it appears. Not that we were quarrelling. I did not have any real concerns with James. I do not still. He was still the most handsome man I had met, still wealthy enough to keep me comfortable, and challenging, in that there was room for him to be challenged. I knew I was not destined for docility, regardless of my protestations, but was I destined for contentment? Would I always be disconsolate? I could not even understand *why* this feeling was haunting me on my wedding day, but it had affixed itself to me much like a shadow. If the wedding itself could not promise joy, then what hope had we for our future? Perhaps I should have married Ann? That is rather less glib a comment than it sounds. We were the happy couple that had danced together that day. James and I were too busy wading through the weeds of domestic drear to remember to have any fun.

But then what else was there? Was a flirtation with Edward ever anything but a whiff of fantasy built from a pile of falsehoods? Edward was at worst a bored man, at best a weak one. The tongue of a poet in the mouth of the craven. He spoke as though willing to flout convention, but it was James with his plodding determination to wed, his fixed plans of where we go at which point, that had built a career from independent, adventurous bold moves. Strong, assertive, daring. Yet I only witnessed the conventional side: giving orders or presenting expectations. Why did he not discuss these bold moves with me? Could we not have made bold moves together?

We stayed in England for a few weeks. It barely seemed enough time to really decorate the space we were in or be intentional about anything. We talked back and forth but mostly travelled around the UK, using the cottage as our base. I wanted to show him parts of Great Britain he had not yet seen. And I wanted him to meet Mary Forbes. We went to Scotland, but she was not there at the time. I wrote a letter to Alice, just updating her really, just keeping the correspondence going. And then somehow, despite all of the back and forth and the thinking, the days raced on and suddenly it was the night before I was to go.

I had plans to meet the Queen.

I got into my brougham, and on the way we were stopped by another. I had a terrible feeling that this was what it was to be attacked in one's carriage. But instead, there was some conversation between the two men commanding the horses. I sat straight, my mouth a grim line as I awaited my fate. How unfortunate for poor James that this wedding gift he gave me – a superfluous one at that, as who needs a brougham with a coachman and a crest when they would soon be leaving the place it could be useful – would prove so deadly. At the very least, how do men become coachmen now, if anyone can be bribed to take their mistress astray?

Edward climbed into my brougham, and presumably they had already discussed where we were to go. Because we went in a different direction from the palace, and from Edward's seat. Or perhaps we came to a different part of it, given how confidently he stepped out onto the green. It was dark and the smattering of stars illuminated the otherwise opaque sky. I could feel the wind against my neck and under my arms. And now that we were out and there was no one to overhear us, he spoke.

"I cannot promise you anything," were the first words out of his mouth. "I am the firstborn. And I am conditioned to a life I did not choose. I think you know that I love you. You know that there is nowhere in this world where the sun will rise and the sun will set and in the time between I will not have reflected on the love that I have for this woman who has gone beyond my reach. I do not wish that to be my every day. I do not want to live steeped in regret. I cannot pretend that I can offer you something. But I cannot fathom never seeing you again. You are married. I am to be married. I think I can live, if only so we might have moments like this, where we might speak. I do not wish to be your friend. I do not ask you to be indiscreet. I am not making an untoward demand. I want to call upon you at the palace and look upon you and remind myself of what I have lost. I want to be reminded of what it is to love – what it is to *live* – and why. It is improper and unfair and foolhardy of me to ask, but time is of the essence and I will not get another chance. Can I ask you to stay? Would you remain here and not go so far out of reach that I will never see or hear from one who even knows your name? Or where you might live or what your address might be? Would you stay?"

He looked so young. Naivety made flesh under the soft veneer of polished entitlement. I am a woman. I had no patience for the frivolities of fantasy or the earnest urges of clumsy, uncertain men.

I would not settle for a man, or a world, that sought to capture me without a sense of their own clarity first. He stood watching my mouth with breathless hesitation.

17 September 1862
Somewhere on the seas
Exact location unknown

I was a married woman led by a betrothed nobleman out of her brougham and into the dark autumn night. I could hear his breathing, could sense the imperceptible shifts in the air. He had been careful just to gesture that I accompany him out on the green, but any moment now, he would reach forth, and taking my silence as assent, attempt to take my hand.

"Edward," I paused, "you do realize I was *on my way somewhere?*"

He spluttered.

It was too dark for him to see my smile. "I have a meeting with the Queen of this country, of the British Empire, which you have obstructed. Or simply made me late for."

"I did not mean..."

"To delay me? Were you hoping to stall me entirely?"

"Bonetta—"

"I have a title. What I lack is time."

"Of course, shall I—"

"And the appetite for this conversation."

Did he think I was taking my brougham for a jaunt on the night before I was to leave? That I had left my husband at home, before the greatest voyage of our lives, for fripperies? He had not considered it. Why? Because all he could think of was his need.

Only a man would deem a woman's plans forgettable in the face of his immediate impulse. A man or a monarch.

"Princess ... Mrs Davies, forgive me, please." Edward opened the carriage door and I took my seat inside. I looked out and watched him talking to my coachman. "Please escort Mrs Davies to Windsor Castle at once," he insisted, in an imperial tone.

He strode back to the carriage door, opened it and stepped in. *The gall.*

"You are not joining. I have no appetite for the inappropriate either."

He stopped half-seated in an awkward squat. I almost laughed. But I was angry. And this was not the important conversation I needed to have today.

"You have a brougham waiting right over there!" I snapped, turning away as the shame spread over his face. As the door closed behind him, I leaned out of my window and shouted out to my coachman. It was unbecoming of a lady to do such a thing, but this same coachman had facilitated this silly late-night tryst, which I had not sought. He had been hired by James. My reputation could have been besmirched by one word about this encounter from the coachman to anyone, but most of all James. How tawdry a world might I have ended up in, having to bribe my own coachman to keep my night-time meetings secret from my husband when I had done nothing untoward? I had long since felt bad for never learning the man's name. I did not then. He should have been relieved. I am certain I could have had him imprisoned or otherwise for bribery. Perhaps even worse, anything could have happened that night. Surely facilitating that is an offence for which he would be punished. Not that orchestrating his punishment was at the forefront of my mind. Upon reflection, he was fortunate that I merely instructed him in blunt tones to proceed forth with haste.

Edward's detour had brought me further from my original course but closer in practice to Windsor Castle. His family's estate is in Surrey Hills, and while it had been too dark to be precise about a place I had been less than a handful of times, it seemed plausible enough that he would intercede and redirect us to location at his convenience.

The journey between Clifton Hill in Brighton, where James and I had made our home this summer, and the castle in Windsor, which had been an informal secondary home for me for almost ten years, was quite so long it always required an overnight stay or a change in brougham; the distance was rather too much for any single coachman and horse. Ordinarily I would proffer without being asked and encourage the coachman to find himself suitable lodgings for the night after depositing me somewhere amenable. I had intended to stay with a childhood friend of Princess Alice, newly wed to the wealthy third son of a baron who lived near to Guildford. I would have travelled to the castle the following morning and met with the Queen before breakfast. I had come to assume monarchy to be indolent in nature, fond of their sleep, keen to rest and enjoy languid mornings awake in bed – with the exception of the late Prince Albert, who I suspect rose early even on his birthday. But in any case, it meant fewer staff would be awake at that time and thus fewer obstacles to our conversation.

The coachman had the audacity to disagree. He had climbed down and walked over to my carriage window and said in broad unabashed tones, "I cannot continue tonight, Mrs Davies. It is another thirty miles or so and the horses have already done more than that. They need to rest."

My eyes narrowed. *He* was tired, for which I cared little. Edward was still outside, waiting perhaps to see what the commotion was about. I opened my carriage door against the coachman's chest and he staggered back, looking shocked. Looking back, I think that it was because I was leaving, or perhaps I decided that pleasing myself was reason enough, or maybe I was tired of being sabotaged by monarchs and men and wished to act with as much empathy as they did. I still cannot fathom what possessed me, but I remember my body marching out of the carriage and walking round to Edward, who was hurriedly getting into his own carriage as I approached.

"Stop."

He turned around.

"You have inconvenienced me."

I could see the whites of his widened eyes gleaming in the darkness. His mouth opened with uncertainty. He was not sure how to proceed. He waited for a cue from me. Were this a Charlotte Brontë novel, I would be resolved to accompany Edward to his family's home, where he might chastely but determinedly win me over once more. But this is my diary recounting my actual journey and I can still all but taste the impatience within me from that evening.

"My carriage cannot take me to Windsor."

"Ah. Well. My carriage can escort you—"

"To Windsor?"

My coachman let out a low whistle.

I ignored him.

"Well, I had meant..." Edward faltered. "That can be arranged."

"I do not need your carriage. I have a carriage."

"You just said..."

"I just told yer—" The coachman walked over, interrupting.

"That the horses need to rest. You do not."

His lips flapped, soundlessly gaping.

"My h-horses? But not the carriage?" Edward stuttered.

"That is correct."

"But…"

"You will unhook your horses from your carriage – both coach-men can assist. You will do the same to mine. You will swap. Your horses will take me in my carriage thirty miles to Windsor Castle tonight. And my new coachman here shall drive."

Edward and the coachman looked at each other.

"Do it. Now."

Was it overcomplicated and unnecessary? It was. Had I inconve-nienced them both to serve my whims? I had indeed. Was this not the behaviour of both men immediately prior? Did *my* coachman not agree to veer off our journey for whatever fee Edward's had paid him? He had indeed. They inconvenienced women for money or their mood, never granting it more than a moment's reflection.

Now they would.

Or rather, that is what I tell myself now. At the time, my satisfac-tion was rather self-serving. I had one person left I needed to see. And as the coachman finished connecting Edward's horses and I climbed into the carriage, I braced myself for the journey, for the drive that would take all night.

To see the Queen.

1 October 1862
Somewhere on the seas
Exact location unknown

I have drawn out the events of two days in August over several pages and entries of this diary. I shall continue writing in this little book, why would I not? A life does not end because one leaves England, despite what the Englishman may say. But those events denote the last days I spent in England and, in light of how far the country is from where I am going and how long it would take to return, I write with a sense of finality. I do consider the 'goodbye' that I said to be for good. I have, without doubt, such an excess of reflections and feelings that they have dragged the story of my departure across too many hours of writing and recollecting. But I do also have the rolling seas to contend with, and moments of quiet are so few and far between. I think back to the ship that first brought me to British shores, to the reputation I so quickly attained for my apparent poise and intellect. Who can maintain poise when a ship is lurching around like so? In truth I cannot believe I spent so many months on ships. I am ill-equipped to travel this way. I am so overcome with sickness, it engulfs me every day. And so I can only write on good days, when both the sky and mind are clear and bright and the ship cuts its way through the waves so smoothly I can stand like I am on solid ground.

On such days, I can not only write, but think back; I can reflect.

As the carriage rolled down the Long Walk, past the dotted trees to the George IV Gateway, I was reminded of that birthday trip I took to the castle, accompanied by the Reverend and Elizabeth on foot, having arrived by train. It was almost exactly two years before; it was in the same month of August. But it was 1860, back when having a tea party on my birthday was my biggest concern.

Before the carriage pulled right up to the gates, I ordered it to stop and jumped out.

Usually they would take me through to the Inner Hall, but I knew at this time of night the footmen would be alarmed. At that point it was so very late and I was so very tired. I was keen for everything to proceed as peacefully as possible.

It was pitch black outside; I could not see the ground under my feet, but it felt familiar. I knew the castle. I knew my place.

The tired footmen at the gate greeted me with surprise. "Were we expecting you, Miss Forbes Bonetta?"

"Princess," the other footman corrected him, pointedly.

"Mrs Davies is fine." I smiled and continued. "There is no formal arrangement for me to visit today; however, I do have to see Her Majesty and I would rather not wait out here in the cold and dark."

"Yes…" The first footman looked flustered. I could see the panic on his face. How to both escort me all the way to the Upper Ward *and* arrange for somebody to prepare a room for me when most of the staff were asleep? He could not leave his post for quite that long.

I almost felt pity for him. I had not planned to create this much inconvenience. He took me all the way to the Upper Ward, but as he ventured towards the apartments favoured by the Queen, he hesitated again. I watched as he silently attempted to work out where it might be best to place me, which housekeeping staff would be up soonest, and before he could put forth an ill-advised plan, I said, "I know my way."

"To … where?"

I looked at him.

"Not Her Majesty's bedchamber!" He gasped like I had confessed to arranging the Gunpowder Plot.

No, of course not. But what I said was, "She will not be sleeping, not at this time."

"Well…"

"Since the passing of His Royal Highness Prince Albert, you must know, she rarely sleeps."

"Ye-es."

"I shall be boarding a ship this evening." *It was not technically true. I would be departing the following day, but these were mere details…*

"A ship where?" the footman asked, then placed a hand over his mouth and shook his head.

I raised my brows for less than a moment, my mouth twitched. "Everywhere."

I went to wait in the Queen's favourite Drawing Room having sent the nervous footman back to his post. I found the scullery maid cleaning the fireplace and instructed her to send for a lady's maid, who could in turn send for the Queen. As she gulped and hurried off, I almost laughed at the inefficiency of it all, remembering how I had wanted a lady's maid of my own back when I lived with the Schoens. How much time had I spent longing for petty trifles to make me feel loved, or simply alive? I sighed and traced a hand over the deep burgundy wallpaper, so muted and enduring against the explosions of gold that framed everything else, from the paintings to the gilded edges of the furniture. Two years ago I longed to be the bright and gilded flower, perpetually in bloom.

The Queen arrived.

She looked small, rumpled and, from afar, like a young child again, but with wrinkles bathing her eyes. She was heavier in her grief. It clung to her, a literal weight that held on tightly, walking with her as she moved. As she walked further into the room, I could see she was dressed in nightclothes that were far too large and long for her. They belonged to Prince Albert.

"Do you recall your first night here, Bonetta?" she asked me, her voice scratchy from a lack of sleep.

"I was just thinking about it. It was the first time I saw you in your nightclothes."

"I put the crown away quickly." She was wistful. "I wanted you to see me at your bedtime. I thought you might be afraid."

"I was afraid."

"I thought so." She sighed. "I thought you would need a queen, but one who could be a protector, who knew what it was to be afraid."

"I think you wore his nightclothes then, as well." I dared not say his name. Not yet.

She closed her eyes. Her steps had slowed, and she reached out to the nearest chaise for support and sat heavily on to it. "I suspect I did."

I did not know how I felt, but a furrow crossed my brow. "Such efforts you made at the start."

She stared at me, aghast. "Sally?"

"You would not have said goodbye. Since my wedding you have neither summoned me nor sent a wedding gift. You spent *all* that time with James before we were betrothed; you will have known that his plan was to return to Africa as soon as he could once the marriage ceremony was complete. Would I have set sail with nary a word passing between us? Would we have spoken ever again?"

"Sally." Her voice was reproachful now, but softer. I could hear the guilt.

"I cannot empathize with you, not until I have made space to honour my own feelings first." I walked over to where she sat, closing the distance between us and pulling an upholstered chair after me.

I crossed my legs at the ankles and sat down slowly. "I remember it so well, the year you forgot my birthday. I was given a diary as a gift and so I recorded it. You were the only person I knew who kept a diligent diary, books filled with your reflections of the day. I was reading mine yesterday morning. Everything else had been packed away for the voyage. I realized something, something I had not previously known."

She was silent but nodded me on.

"At the time, the only thing I had was my voice. I felt certain that to assert it was to demonstrate independence, womanhood. Yet at the same time, I was desperate to find someone to whom I appeared to matter. Not as a trinket, not because of my race or in spite of it, not because of my intellect or any known quality. Regardless of any such attributes. I did not understand then, but that is what it means to belong. It is how you create it in others or are raised with it in oneself. What does it mean to belong? Well, it contains that contradiction, whereby you are able to seek independence because you are valued by those around you. To carry within a sense that you are loved, that you matter, just by existing … it is emboldening. And it is the foundation upon which a healthy kind of independence can be built. I wanted you to tell me I belonged."

"Sally, you did, you always did!"

"I wanted you to tell me I belonged because then I could finally be free."

The Queen looked stricken. "Sally, I could never give you that kind of upbringing; how could I? One has to feel it, to be able to offer it to others. Albert was always the better parent – to our children, at least. He knew what it was to be loved. He could offer it to them..." She hiccoughed as she spoke.

I heard, rather than saw, her tears. "I do not have much more to say to you, Your Majesty. But Brighton..." It was my turn to take a deep breath. "Brighton..." I could not get much further.

Something shifted in her expression. "But you are happy with James, are you not?"

"Am I happy?"

"Sally..."

"James treats me well. Very well." *So far.* I paused. "But am I happy with him? The question is, will I ever feel happiness again?"

"And the answer is—"

"And the reason it is a question, is because of Brighton." I rose to my feet. Outside the sky has shifted from pitch black to the patchy pale pink of sunrise. It streamed in through the full-length windows, announcing the new day. I suddenly felt sleepy. Despite the arduous journey to get to the castle, I wanted nothing more than to get back.

I curtsied to my queen.

She stared up at me, tear tracks stained on those apple cheeks of hers. "You are leaving, fleeing England, because of Brighton, because of me?"

A year ago, I would have been confused or upset at the selfish inaccuracies of her conclusion. But I did not need my life to make sense to her. I was not waiting for her validatory seal. I did not need another's gaze to humanize me.

"Your Majesty," I said, my tone genial, "I am a young bride with a seafaring husband and neither of us was born in this country. We are not fleeing, we are seeking, searching for pastures new." And pastures old, to find the traces of our histories.

Why, after all, am I really still writing in this diary? So that I can bear witness. So that I can see. It is written for me.

And with that, I left the room, left Windsor Castle and stepped out into the light.

Timeline

1807 Abolition of the Slave Trade Act makes it illegal to buy and sell enslaved people in British colonies. However, it does not free people who are already enslaved.

1st August 1834 The Slavery Abolition Act (1833) comes into effect in most British colonies, in which the British government bought the freedom of 800,000 enslaved people. The British government sets up the Slave Compensation Commission and pays out (to the slaveowners) 40% of the national budget, 20 million pounds back then, equivalent to 17 billion pounds today. The government borrows the money from financial institutions to make this payment. The British public are made to pay back the loan, through their taxes. These payments continue until 2015.

20 June 1837 18-year-old Victoria becomes Queen of the United Kingdom of Great Britain and Ireland.

10 February 1840 Queen Victoria marries her German cousin,

Albert. The marriage is a love match and it is thought that Victoria proposed to Albert, which was highly unusual at that time.

Approx. 1843 Omo'ba Aina is born in Oke-Odan in what is now Nigeria, West Africa. Her father is a tribal chief.

1848 King Gezo of Dahomey's army attacks Oke-Odan, killing Aina's parents and taking her captive. (Dahomey is now part of present-day Benin.)

July 1850 Captain Frederick Forbes of the HMS Bonetta travels to Dahomey on a diplomatic mission. King Gezo gives Aina to him as a gift for Queen Victoria.

July/August 1850 Captain Forbes has Aina baptised as Sarah Forbes Bonetta, named after himself and his ship, in the port of Badagry (Nigeria). Sarah travels with him to England.

9 November 1850 Sarah is presented to Queen Victoria at Windsor Castle, who describes her as 'sharp and intelligent'.

May 1851 Sarah returns to Africa due to poor health. She attends the Church Missionary Society school in Freetown, Sierra Leone. Sarah's education is paid for by Queen Victoria, who sends her regular letters and small gifts, such as toys and books.

1851 Captain Forbes publishes *Dahomey and the Dahomans*, an account of his mission to Dahomey, that includes details about Sarah.

4 June 1852 Captain Forbes dies aboard HMS *Tortoise*, en route to the island of St Helena.

September 1855 Queen Victoria orders Sarah's return to England. Now aged 12, Sarah goes to live with the Schoen family, former missionaries, in Chatham, Kent.

December 1855 Sarah visits Queen Victoria at Windsor Castle.

January 1858 Sarah attends the wedding of Queen Victoria's eldest daughter, Victoria.

Spring 1861 West African businessman James Pinson Labulo Davies asks eighteen year-old Sarah to marry him. Sarah refuses and is sent to live in Brighton.

14 December 1861 Prince Albert, Queen Victoria's husband, dies of typhoid fever.

1862 Sarah's friend Princess Alice (Queen Victoria's third child) marries the German Prince Louis of Hesse.

14 August 1862 With Queen Victoria's permission, Sarah marries James Davies in a ceremony officiated by the Bishop of Sierra Leone. She has 16 bridesmaids and signs her name as 'Aina Sarah Forbes Bonetta' on her marriage certificate.

Late 1862 Sarah and her husband return to Africa, initially to Sierra Leone.

1863 Sarah gives birth to her first child, Victoria. Queen Victoria gives her namesake a gold cup, salver, knife, fork and spoon, and agrees to be her protector.

December 1867 Sarah travels to England with her daughter and visits Queen Victoria at Windsor Castle. It's the last time they see each other.

Late 1860s Sarah is diagnosed with tuberculosis, a bacterial infection that was incurable at that time.

1871 Sarah gives birth to a son, Arthur.

1873 Sarah's daughter, Stella, is born.

1880 Sarah's health is deteriorating, and she travels to Madeira in the hope that the warm climate will help her.

15 August 1880 Sarah Forbes Bonetta dies of tuberculosis in Funchal, Madeira, at the age of thirty-seven. Queen Victoria hears the news on the day that Sarah's daughter, Victoria, is due to visit her.

1881/83 Queen Victoria pays for her godchild and namesake to be educated at Cheltenham Ladies College. They remain in contact.

22 January 1901 Queen Victoria dies at Osborne House on the Isle of Wight. At that time, she is the longest-serving monarch in British history.

2015 Britain finally finished paying off the loan the government took out to compensate the slaveowners after the 1833 Slavery Abolition Act.

ACKNOWLEDGEMENTS

To Walter Dean Myers, John Van der Kiste & Adeyemo Elebute without whose works listed below, in order of relevance, I could not have written this one.

At Her Majesty's Request: An African Princess in Victorian England

Sarah Forbes Bonetta: Queen Victoria's African Princess

The Life of James Pindon Labulo Davies: A Colossus of Victorian Lagos

Thank you for giving me the capacity to furnish this story, my fictional account of her diary with your tireless research, commitment to detail and compassionate but unflinching account of life at that time. And your painstaking accuracy. Thank you for ensuring Sarah Forbes Bonetta's story was not forgotten.

The Diary of Sarah Forbes Bonetta: A Novel wouldn't have been possible without the tireless efforts of Maria, Anna, Clara and Leah – and everyone at Pontas and Scholastic involved with the making of this book. Leah and everyone at Scholastic in particular, I thank you for your tremendous patience throughout it all, your empathy and encouragement, on the journey to completing it.

I also thank you all for your much needed assessments and perspectives on the story. Every editor and fact checker who gave each line and each word such focus and care; you have had an incalculable impact on the execution and delivery of this.

Without your guidance, *The Diary of Sarah Forbes Bonetta: A Novel* may well look quite different. And that would be to its detriment.

To my mother and those loved ones who remain my biggest supporters and continue to urge me on to fulfil all my personal goals, who supported through this, you know who you are – I thank you.

I'm proud of this book. It was not a solo endeavour. As all novelists know, writing books never is. But bringing this to fruition has been a long-held personal desire of mine, it is the book my adolescent self dreamed of reading. Thank you to all of you for making that a reality.